Kingston Libraries

On line Services

www.kingston.gov.uk/libraries

Renew a book (5 times)
Change of address
Library news and updates
Search the catalogue

Request a book
Find a branch
Get your pin
reference sites

KT-416-380

8547 5006

FUNNY BY NAME,
FUNNY BY NATURE

TOP SECRET

FROM THE GOVERNMENT DEPARTMENT
OF TOP SECRETS

If you are reading this, it means that you've gained access to one of the worst kept secrets in the history of the secret service.

Before continuing, I need you to carefully check that no one is reading over your shoulder—go ahead, do it now.

First off, that was terrible, really obvious. If I'm going to tell you top secret government information, you're going to have to be a bit more stealthy. Try again.

Was anyone looking? No? Right, then I'll begin.

This year the Secret Service made a major mix-up: they mistook a 13-year-old boy called Kevin for a secret agent. (I know, so much for an 'intelligence' agency.)

CONFIDENTIAL

This was the sort of kid that would try to zip-wire across a building and end up falling head first into a fountain with his bum on show, so can you imagine what happened when he was allowed access to the amazing sort of spy gadgets that James Bond would use?

Despite this, it was up to Kevin to save us all from an evil supervillain. It was the most dangerous, daring mission in the history of the Secret Service, and also its biggest blunder.

This official document uncovers the entire story of Kevin's fateful* mission.

WARNING!
AS SOON AS YOU TURN THE PAGE THE COUNTDOWN BEGINS.
THIS BOOK WILL SELF-DESTRUCT IN 230 PAGES.

*and utterly hilarious

To my editor Clare,
for all her help and encouragement

OXFORD
UNIVERSITY PRESS

Great Clarendon Street, Oxford OX2 6DP
Oxford University Press is a department of the University of Oxford.
It furthers the University's objective of excellence in research, scholarship,
and education by publishing worldwide

Oxford is a registered trade mark of Oxford University Press
in the UK and in certain other countries

Text and illustration © Tom McLaughlin 2016
The moral rights of the author and illustrator have been asserted

Database right Oxford University Press (maker)

First published 2016

British Library Cataloguing in Publication Data

Data available

ISBN: 978-0-19-274439-5

1 3 5 7 9 10 8 6 4 2

Printed in Great Britain
Paper used in the production of this book is a natural,
recyclable product made from wood grown in sustainable forests
The manufacturing process conforms to the environmental
regulations of the country of origin.

THE Accidental
SECRET AGENT

Written and illustrated by

Tom
McLaughlin

OXFORD
UNIVERSITY PRESS

EVERYBODY WAS KUNG-FU FIGHTING

'Ladies and gentlemen, we have spent a lifetime hiding in the shadows but today we finally get what we've all been waiting for. For today is Judgement Day. I look around this room and it makes me proud.' Mr X paused to puff on a large cigar.

'Look at the great things we've already done. We steal, not to make us rich, but because we can. We hurt, not because we're scared, but because we're courageous. And today, we destroy the world!'

Knowing nods rippled around the room, which

corrupt politicians, ghastly gangsters, and vile villains.

'We are finally ready,' said Mr X, sitting at the end of the very long table. 'All I need to do is press this red button and—'

'PIZZA!' a chirpy voice interrupted. Everyone turned to see the crash-helmeted pizza delivery boy, craning round the door. The smell of piping hot cheese and warm cardboard filled the room.

'I've got PIIIIIIIIIZZA!' he cheerfully called.

'I'm sorry, there appears to be some sort of mistake. I didn't order any . . .' Mr X said, scratching his head.

'Do you have ham and pineapple?' an assassin called the Black Widow chipped in (that wasn't her real name; her real name was Doris, but Doris the assassin would sound silly). 'I could go for a bit of ham and pineapple.'

'Ew,' Ivan the Even Worse interrupted. 'Fruit *and* meat together? I find that so weird.'

Mr X raised his voice. 'Please don't eat any pizza. If you eat it, they make you pay for it. I know how these people work.'

'I like it,' the Black Widow said, staring at Ivan the Even Worse.

'I'll say it again. FRUIT AND MEAT TOGETHER! You're insane.'

'We're all insane. That's why we're here—we're about to destroy the world. Now if you don't stop making fun of me, I'll have to kill you to death,' the Black Widow snarled.

'Mr X, Mr X!' Ivan called out, putting his hand up, 'she threatened to kill me to death.'

'Can we all shut up?!' Mr X screamed. 'I didn't order pizza, nor did anyone else. I have a selection of light nibbles and some squash prepared for when we've finished throwing the world into a black hole of insanity, but until then, nothing,' he said, looking at the kid in the motorcycle helmet.

'Sure you did. You've got your margherita, your ham and pineapple, yeah . . .' he said, giving a thumbs-up to the Black Widow. 'And we've got your stuffed crust of whoop-ass. Now, did you want that with extra karate chops?' he said, opening the lid.

'What . . . ?' Mr X said, peering into the box.

The pizza delivery boy swung his fist through the bottom of the box, knocking Mr X out cold. Quick as a flash, the rest of the assembled baddies started reaching into their pockets to pull out any weapon they could find. But before their fingers even reached pocket lint, the delivery boy had frisbee'd the pizzas across the room, instantly taking out half a dozen of the hapless horribles. A general pulled a machine gun from his sock, but before he had the chance to take aim, the delivery boy had reached into his side bag and whipped out a bottle of cola, shaking it vigorously, and opening it up, sending a stream of foamy fizzy pop right at the general's face.

'AAAAARGGGGH!' the general screamed. 'My eyes!'

'Oh, I'm sorry. Do you prefer it stirred, not shaken?' the delivery boy asked.

'Amateurs,' the Black Widow shrieked, pulling out her nunchucks and spinning them round her head. 'Time to let the grown-ups have a play.'

'Oh, you wanna play, do you?' the delivery boy replied, pulling down his visor. He reached inside his pizza bag, pulled out a couple of garlic baguettes, and twirled them so fast all the Black Widow could see was a bready blur. 'Oh yeah, that's it, drink it in, this is how I roll.' He flung a garlic baguette straight at the Black Widow, striking her to the ground.

'Who . . . who are you?' Mr X asked shakily.

The delivery boy pulled off his helmet and shook his hair back in place. There stood a boy, I mean a real boy; he couldn't have been more than thirteen years old. Mr X couldn't believe his eyes.

'The name's Twigg. Kevin Twigg. Licence to get all up in your face.'

'What?'

'Oh, I think you heard me, you bag of plums.'

'I beg your pardon?! WHO ARE YOU CALLING A BAG OF PLUMS? See me after assembly, Twigg.'

'Twigg?'

'TWIGG?!'

'Are you listening to me?'

Kevin snapped out of his daydream and sat up with a jolt, dropping the games console he had been playing on. He wasn't fighting baddies. Kevin was in assembly and in big trouble. The whole of his year were all craning their necks to look at him and there, at the front, stood Mr Plunk. He was Kevin's elderly headmaster, a spindly man who looked as if he was made of string and bad moods.

'Oh, sorry, sir,' Kevin said, his face burning puce with shame.

'What's that in your hand?' the headmaster snapped.

'Erm, a calculator, Mr Plunk!' Kevin replied

immediately. He decided to take a chance because the headmaster was very old and there was a possibility that he wouldn't know the difference between a games console and a calculator.

'I'm not an idiot, Kevin. I know a blasted computer when I see one. Awful things, with their internet and funny cat videos . . .' he snarled. 'I'll see you afterwards, Twigg. Now open your ears and pay attention!'

Twenty minutes later Kevin filed out of morning assembly, the embarrassment still hanging over him like a cloud.

'Hey, Twigg. Can I see your licence to "get all up in my face"?' one kid laughed.

'Well done, Kevin. You find new and interesting ways to be a moron every day,' another bellowed, before punching him in the arm. Kevin desperately tried to rub the sting away without letting anyone know that it hurt. His head felt like a washing machine of bad thoughts, each one spinning round and round on a never-ending cycle. *Why did he always have to get carried away, pretending he was the secret agent*

in the movie of his life? Why couldn't he just play his games console in secret like the other boys instead of going off into a mad daydream and shouting about getting all up in someone's face? Kevin imagined life without being yelled at by teachers before realizing that he was daydreaming about not daydreaming.

'Man, you have to be more careful,' Pete whispered loudly into his ear. 'You know Mr Plunk has it in for you.'

'Pete's right. I bet you were in your own world, fantasizing about being Ninja Pizza Boy again, weren't you?' Stu said, shaking his head.

Pete and Stu were Kevin's two best friends, which was a good job as they were also Kevin's only friends. They'd practically spent their whole lives together. All the way from nursery to big school. They were a little gang of misfits, with Kevin as their misfit-in-chief.

'Well, it was good while it lasted. I just want to do something cool with my life. I bet I'd make a really good secret agent,' Kevin pondered. 'I'm practically fluent in ninja. I'm pretty sure I could take down a real baddie with one arm tied behind my back.'

'Who has ever heard of a thirteen-year-old secret agent?' Stu asked. 'Especially one with athlete's foot and a cheese problem.'

'OK, firstly, the infection on my foot has cleared up now, and secondly, I don't have a cheese problem!' Kevin barked.

'What do you have in your lunch box, Kev?' Pete asked.

'Nothing. Just a sandwich and an apple and a chocolate bar,' Kevin said casually.

'What else?' Stu said, raising an eyebrow.

'That's it. Nothing else,' Kevin said, shuffling his feet and avoiding eye contact.

'Keviiiiiiin?' Stu said, nudging him.

'OK, OK, SOME CHEDDAR AND A SMALL LUMP OF BRIE. MY NAME'S KEVIN AND I LOVE CHEESE! HAPPY NOW?'

Kevin blurted at Pete and Stu, laughing.

'A computer-loving cheese addict, huh, Twigg? Not got a lot going for you, have you, boy? No wonder your brainbox has turned to dribble.' It was the headmaster again. He grabbed Kevin by the earlobe, yanking him along the corridor as he hollered at him.

'Arrrgh, no . . . NO!' yelled Kevin. 'I was just saying how right you were, sir. Computers are nothing but trouble.'

Mr Plunk narrowed his eyes. 'Yes, yes, they are stupid, aren't they,' he said, looking off into the distance. 'One day this fad for all things electronical will come to a crashing end. What's wrong with a blackboard and chalk? It was good enough for me back in my day! Now get back to lessons, Twigg, you snivelling little weasel. Order, manners, and a civilized world, that's what we need.' And, with that, he glided off down the corridor, barking at other children as he went.

'Wow, he really hates computers, doesn't he?' Stu said, looking puzzled.

'Yeah,' Kevin nodded. 'I wonder why. Do you think his pet dog was crushed by a laptop or something?' Kevin watched suspiciously as Mr Plunk shut his office door behind him. 'Do you think it's odd—' Kevin began.

'No!' yelled Pete.

'What?' Kevin said. 'You don't know what I was about to say.'

'Yes, we do,' Stu joined in. 'You were going to say something about Mr Plunk being up to something. Like he's an evil mastermind or that he goes around using puppies as slippers or something.'

'No . . .' Kevin said, looking awkward. They walked a few more steps down the corridor, then Kevin couldn't keep it in any longer. 'All I was going to say was, don't you think it's strange that no one has ever been hauled into Mr Plunk's office, considering how he's always telling us all off and everything. I mean, I wonder what he's up to in there.'

'I knew it. I knew it!' Pete said, rolling his eyes. 'You always do this, Kevin; you always think that there's a mystery to be solved, a crime to be cracked. I swear sometimes you don't know what's real or what's fantasy.' Pete shook his head.

'If you think I'm that weird, I suppose you won't want to come round and play on my new MiPhone25 then?' Kevin said triumphantly.

'You don't have one,' Stu replied.

'Well, no, not yet. But I will soon. I'm saving up all my money and after tonight, I reckon I'll be really close . . .'

'OK, OK, I'll ask,' Pete said, with an air of regret in his voice. 'What's happening tonight?'

'Glad you asked, Pete, old buddy. Tonight I will be putting on the stunt show to end all stunt shows,' Kevin said, grinning. 'I shall be zip-wiring from the rooftops in town, before somersaulting over the fountain to rapturous applause, and a hatful of cold, hard cash.'

'You can't do a somersault, Kevin,' Pete sighed.

'Sure I can. I watched the latest James Bond film last night. It looks easy.'

'Watching something on TV does not mean you can do it.'

'Are you sure this is a good idea?' Stu chipped in. 'I mean, you remember what happened last time when you watched sword-swallowing on YouTube? They called you "Kevin the Human Kebab" after that.'

'Oh, stop overreacting. Turns out tonsils aren't that important. Look, just spread the word around the school. I'll see you there at four, by the fountain in town!'

'Are you sure, Kevin?' Pete and Stu both replied.

'I told you, what can possibly go wrong?!'

BIRD ON THE WIRE

Kevin strolled down the street and stopped to admire his reflection in a shop window. You have to look the part if you're going to be flying through the air. Although Kevin *was* having second thoughts about putting on his dad's pants over his mum's tights. He wasn't expecting them to be so baggy, nor so brown. But it was too late now, and the cape looked pretty good. Kevin checked his watch. He still had a couple of minutes. Just enough time to see it again. Kevin slowly and carefully opened the shop door and crept in.

'DING-A-LING-A-LING' came the bell at the top of the door.

The shop owner, Mr Patel, popped his head up from behind the counter, looked Kevin up and down, and sighed.

'Oooooooh,' he said sadly, 'you know you really didn't need to bother with that ridiculous disguise. I know it's you. I *always* know it's you, Kevin.'

'It's nice to see you too, Mr Patel. Actually I'm not wearing a disguise. This is my costume. You know, for my show. You have to look the business when you're a trained performer like me!' Kevin said, wafting his cape.

'Are you wearing ladies' tights . . . ?' Mr Patel said, scratching his head.

'Never mind that. Can I see it?'

'And old man's pants? Are you wearing another man's pants, Kevin?'

'Just leave it, all right. Can I see it? I haven't got long,' Kevin pleaded.

'No, you can't. I don't have one,' Mr Patel snapped.

'Yes, you do, Mr Patel. I saw it in the window. Pleeeeeease?' Kevin begged.

'You saw it yesterday!'

'Mr Patel, I won't go until I see it!' Kevin insisted, smiling.

'Oh, all right, if you must . . . you know the drill.'

Mr Patel walked over to the glass cabinet by the window. That was where all the newest phones were kept. It's where Kevin could be found most days with his nose pressed against the window. Staring at the MiPhone25. Mr Patel unlocked the cabinet and handed Kevin a pair of white cotton gloves. Kevin slipped them on. It was the only way Kevin was allowed to touch anything in Mr Patel's phone shop these days since 'Marmitegate'. Kevin had come in eating a sticky sandwich and made rather a lot of mess all over a new shipment of smartphones from Korea.

'You know the rules. No gaming. No comedy ringtones . . .'

'No extreme selfies. Yes, yes, I know. I just want to hold it. Play with its apps a bit.'

'Kevin, have you ever thought that you might be a bit obsessed with phones? And this is coming from a man who owns a phone shop.' Mr Patel looked at Kevin with a special look. Kevin often got the special look. It was a mixture of kindness, sympathy, and worry. But Kevin wasn't listening.

'It's . . . just so wonderful . . . so perfect.' His eyes were glazed and a huge grin stretched out across his face. It was like watching a dog having its belly stroked.

'If you lick it, like you did last week, I'm throwing you out,' Mr Patel warned.

'It tasted of dreams, Mr Patel. Dreams. I bet all the secret agents in the world have one of these. I'd be just like James Bond with this in my hand,' Kevin replied.

'Kevin, I say this as your friend: I like you, but you're deeply, deeply weird. Now put it back. It's not like you can afford one!' Mr Patel said curtly.

'I can't afford it yet,' Kevin said, sniffing it. 'But, after this afternoon, who knows?'

'Ah yes, your show. Are you sure that's a good

idea, after last time? You know, being fired out of a cannon. It didn't work too well.'

'What are you talking about? That was a complete success!'

'Kevin, you landed in a charity shop with your bottom on fire. They called you the Flame-grilled Kevin. You looked like a burnt sausage.'

'That just made it even cooler!' Kevin grinned.

'Some of those poor old ladies in the shop were very scared, Kevin.' Mr Patel shook his head. 'You might get hurt!'

'I'll be fine,' Kevin replied.

'Don't you think you'd be better off living in the real world for once?'

Kevin looked down at his baggy pants and hoicked them up over the tights. 'This time is going to be different, Mr Patel. I'll see you tomorrow.'

'No, you won't. I'm closed. You can't come here.'

'No, you're not, and yes, I will.' Kevin waved as he left.

'Worth a try. OK, see you tomorrow, Kevin.' Mr

Patel smiled begrudgingly, wiping the phone with a hanky.

Kevin headed out of the shop and round the corner and into a huge crowd of pigeons. *A huge crowd of pigeons? Where were all his fans?* Kevin spotted Stu and Pete. Well, let's be honest, it wasn't hard.

'Where is everyone?!' Kevin yelled.

'Don't look at us!' Pete said. 'We did our best, we told everyone . . .'

'Yeah, we even made posters,' Stu chipped in, pulling one out of his bag so Kevin could see.

'Kevin's world famous *stump* show . . . ?' Kevin read.

'No—it says stunt.'

'That's not an 'n' or a 't', is it?'

'Yeah, of course it is.'

'Oh boy . . .' Kevin sighed as he looked out at the town square. There was Stu, Pete, and the strange kid from the year below them (the one who never went swimming because he had a funny ear). Then there were two girls from Kevin's class, who were giggling, but in a mean way, holding a sign which read:

R.I.P. KEVIN KEBAB BOY

Alongside them was an old woman, who was sitting on the bench, feeding the pigeons chips from the local KFC, and a cat, who was asleep.

Except, that wasn't quite everybody. There was another person there too. A man, lurking in the shadows out of sight. He was lost in his own thoughts, staring at the phone in his hand and hoping beyond all hope that it didn't ring. If only he could be normal, he thought. If only he could be like everyone else. He gazed around at the passers-by. A woman feeding the birds. Normal. A couple of school kids. There was a beauty in their everyday-ness. A boy in pants and tights. Normal. Wait, that's not normal! The man looked again, but his

concentration was broken by the sound of the phone ringing. He crumpled into a heap on the floor. It was them. It was always them.

'Roll up, roll up!' Kevin bellowed in a voice too loud for such small crowd. 'It's time for the greatest show on earth. It's time for Kevin's World Famous Stunt Show!'

'It says stump . . .' the woman feeding the pigeons said.

'No, it doesn't, that's quite clearly an "n" and a "t" . . . Never mind that—the important thing is not the poster, but the show that you're about to see. Today, without the aid of a safety net, without any special harnesses, I shall attempt something that's never been done before. I shall zip-wire from the top of the pound shop, across the shopping precinct, before doing a somersault over the fountain next to KFC, and landing perfectly on my feet. They said it couldn't be done . . .'

'Who said that?' the lady piped up again.

'What?' Kevin asked.

'You shouted "they said it couldn't be done". Who is "they"? A health and safety officer? He probably has a point.'

'No, not a health and safety officer, just *they* . . .' Kevin carried on.

'Well, who are these people? Are they some sort of stunt experts, because, unless they are, "they" should keep their opinions to themselves,' the woman huffed.

'Just stop talking. It'd be really helpful if you just stopped the noise coming from your face and let me finish,' Kevin sighed.

'Oh well, that's charming, ain't it. Go on, you go ahead and finish.'

Kevin opened his mouth. 'Oh, I think I had finished.' He took a deep breath. He was really going to do this. He was really going to fly down a zip wire and do a . . .

'Well, get on with it then!' the old woman said, tapping her watch. 'I've got a bus to catch at half past.'

'I'm going, I'm going.' Kevin walked across the pedestrianized square of the shopping precinct. He climbed up the wall next to the bakery and then clambered up to the roof of the pound shop using the fire escape. Kevin emerged triumphantly at the top and waved, flexing his muscles as though he was a superhero.

'WHATEVER YOU DOOOOO,' Pete yelled, 'DON'T LOOK DOWN!'

'WHY, WHAT? AARRRRGH!' Kevin yelled, looking down.

Pete smiled and gave Kevin the thumbs up.

'Why, why would you do that?' Stu asked.

'But I told him not to look down!' Pete protested.

'I swear I'm the only normal one left,' Stu muttered.

Back at the top, Kevin bravely opened one eye. He hadn't realized that it was this high up. *Oh crikey! What if he did a Code Brown in his pants? At least they were quite brown to start with.* Kevin steadied himself against the post holding the wire up and took a deep breath. The wire had been there to hang the bunting from when Kevin's part of town,

Croydon, had come second in 'Tidiest Roundabout in London'. It had narrowly lost out to Hackney, but they did keep the wire up with the bunting on. Possibly as a reminder to the town's great cultural heritage, possibly because no one could be bothered to take it down.

Kevin began to pant and breathe loudly, saying to himself over and over again, 'Be the man, Twigg. Focus!' He began to slap himself in the face—he'd seen it on a film once and wasn't sure why people did it, but it seemed to work in the movies.

'Is he punching himself in the face?' the old woman with the chips asked Stu and Pete.

'Apparently he is,' Stu smiled, before giving Pete a look.

'I think maybe it's part of the show,' Pete added confidently to the old lady.

'Arrrrgh!' came the distant cry as Kevin smacked himself repeatedly around the chops, briefly knocking himself to the ground in the process. He then stopped, stepped forward, and stood at the edge of the building.

All he needed to do was to loop his special rope over the wire and then he would . . . The rope. He'd forgotten the rope!

'Oh, good grief, I've forgotten . . . !' Kevin yelled to Stu and Pete.

'What did he say?' Stu asked out loud, straining to hear Kevin in the distance.

'Something about a rope, but it was hard to tell above the wailing,' Pete replied.

'Ohhh . . . ?' Stu said, scratching his head.

Kevin looked around on the rooftop. There was no way he was going to climb back down. A few more people were watching now. Maybe even as many as twelve. A crowd of that size could easily riot in the face of such disappointment. All he needed was something strong to loop over the wire. Kevin looked down at his belt. He could use his belt. The belt holding his mum's tights up. Normally tights hold themselves up, but his mum had quite big ones so they were a bit baggy around the tummy. Perhaps if Kevin didn't think about his mum's tights falling down, then maybe they wouldn't. *Would that work? It might work*, Kevin pondered to himself. Only one way to find out! Kevin undid the belt and looped it over the wire that stretched from one side of the precinct to another. The tights hadn't fallen down yet. *Perhaps he didn't need the belt after all? Perhaps he was just being over-cautious? Yes, that was it.*

'Oh no. Kevin, what are you doing?' Stu sang under his breath, so as not to cause alarm. 'Put your belt back on. Bad things will happen if you take your belt off.'

Pete looked over at Stu and Stu looked back at Pete. This was going to end badly. The question was, how badly? Front-page-of-the-newspaper-with-a-picture-of-Kevin-stuck-in-a-tree,-his-bare-bottom-showing sort of badly? Or a-prison-sentence badly? Or perhaps some hideous combination of the two.

Kevin looked out over the people and shops below him. He glanced at Mr Patel's shop; he could see the phone gleaming in the window. It was all for that, everything for that. It was totally worth it. He could see Pete and Stu, or at least, he thought it was them. It was hard to tell as they had their heads in their hands. There were a few people from his class. And a man on the phone by the bins. He was probably calling the newspapers or something. Kevin was in the zone. He had his game face on and nothing could distract him now. That was . . . until he saw her. It was as if time stopped. She was the most beautiful thing in the world. She had shoulder-length dark hair that shimmered in the sun and a smile that made Kevin melt. Her eyes were like pools of chocolate: warm chocolate, gooey chocolate. They were the most beautiful chocolatey gooey eyes he'd ever seen. It was as if she had wandered in from a film set . . . *What on earth was someone as beautiful as her doing in a place like this? SHE WAS EVEN PRETTIER THAN A PHONE! Who was she? Had she come to see him?* Kevin stood on his tiptoes to get a better view. Which, it turned out, was a very bad idea. A wobble began, which turned into a tremble, which transformed into a full-scale fall complete with cartoon-style screaming. He looked down at the ground and felt his stomach lurch. He grabbed the belt and threw it over the wire. He caught it with his other

hand just as he hurtled down the bunting. His feet and legs were swinging like a fleshy pendulum. This inevitably made his baggy pants and tights fall down around his ankles. *Of all the days he had to wear his tiger-print undies, why today?* He should be grateful he was wearing any underwear at all. It just felt so weird to double pant at the time, but it was a decision that was paying off now.

Kevin slid towards the fountain at an alarming speed, flying over everyone's heads as they stared open-mouthed in horror. He lifted his knees up to his chest to avoid kicking anyone. At that very second, the mysterious girl turned to look at Kevin. It all happened in slow motion. Kevin gave her his best, hunkiest grin. She did what any girl would do in her situation—she screamed and hit the floor so she didn't get her block knocked off.

It was OK, he was going to be OK! *This was going to be a triumph*, Kevin thought to himself. And he believed it too, right up until the moment his belt got tangled up on the wire and he flew off, spinning head-first towards the fountain. Kevin did not one, not two, but three somersaults. Completely by accident, but they were somersaults all the same.

'WHAAAAAAAAAAEEEEEEEEK!'

he squealed, like a piglet. The crowd covered their ears and winced.

From behind the bins, the man finished his phone call and, alerted to the hullabaloo by the fountain, saw Kevin somersaulting through the air not once, not twice, but three times.

'Wow, is this guy for real? The resemblance is uncanny. The opportunity is just too good to miss. That kid is my ticket out of here!'

Kevin splashed down in the fountain, his belly scraping along the bottom, soggy fast-food wrappers hitting him in the face. He couldn't see a thing, which was probably for the best because it meant he didn't see the wall that was about to hit him in the . . .

'Owwwww, my face!' Kevin yelled. Only underwater, but I don't know how to spell 'Owwww, my face!' being yelled underwater.

By now, Pete and Stu and were flinched in pain for Kevin. The old woman looked at her watch as

Kevin emerged from the
water, peeling KFC fries from
his face.

'You're right,' she said, 'I've never seen anything
like that before.' She sighed, before heading off
to catch her bus, still shaking her head. But Kevin
wasn't interested in what she had to say. He had more
pressing things on his mind.

'Is she here? Did you see her?' Kevin asked Stu
and Pete, as the crowds wandered off, laughing.

'I'm here,' came a girl's voice. 'Sadly for you I did

see it and I'm going to tell Mum and Dad.'

'Elle!' Kevin said in surprise.

'What did I do wrong to be related to you?' she said, eyeing her brother up and down. It was not a pretty sight. He had chicken nuggets stuck to his big lady tights.

'You may be the most embarrassing thing to ever walk this earth. And, as for you two, why don't you stop him?!' She stared at Stu and Pete. They just shrugged and muttered something about a phone. Elle sighed and walked off in disgust.

'Did you see the girl? The one with dark hair?' Kevin said, waiting until his sister was out of earshot. 'I think I'm in love!'

'Oh no,' Stu sighed. 'Kevin, don't you think you should calm down? You're not Ninja Pizza Boy, you're not some International Man of Mystery. You're just Kevin, just plain old Kevin. Why not give being normal a go?' Stu said, trying to be kind, but hurting Kevin's feelings all the same.

Kevin picked up the hat he'd laid down before the show. Twelve pence and what Kevin hoped was a piece of chocolate fudge finger was inside. His latest scheme had failed, along with all the others.

'He's perfect.' The man by the bins grinned. 'Just perfect. The right height, the right hair colour. And pretty nifty on a zip wire too.' The man laughed. 'Goodbye, old life, hello, the new me.'

<u>A note from the author</u>

Hello, it's the author here. It's been pointed out that at this bit of the story, I should add a 'don't try this at home' advisory. Just in case you were thinking of standing on the edge of a tall building and zip-wiring across the town centre. Please don't; none of this is real. Kevin's made of words, and he can't come to any harm. But you're not—you're made of skin and blood and wobbly inside bits and it'd be a shame if any of them got broken. So please, please don't, for goodness' sake, dress in your mum's tights and your dad's pants for a stunt show, in an attempt to get a bit of extra cash to buy a phone that doesn't exist.

Thank you. Much love, Tom x

3

OH HAPPY DAY

Kevin strolled through the park, clutching his tights to stop them falling down, his soppy cape dragging along the ground. He slumped on the nearest bench and put his hat down. A nearby homeless man gave Kevin twenty pence.

'Buy yourself a cup of tea, mate,' he said.

Kevin sighed. This was definitely a new low. 'I look like a drunk Superman, and a homeless person has just give me his last twenty pence. Life is taking the—'

'Pssss!' came a sound from the bushes.

Kevin looked round as a man popped up from behind the shrub and sat on the bench next to him. Well, it looked like a man from what Kevin could see, which was not much. He was holding a giant newspaper in front of his face with two holes cut out for eyes, and next to him was a briefcase. *Was he talking to Kevin? Should he reply? How does one respond to a 'pssss'? Should he 'pssss' back?* Kevin decided to be assertive and say nothing.

'I said, "pssss",' the man said again.

'I know,' whispered Kevin. 'I wasn't really sure how to respond. It wasn't that I was ignoring you, it's just—'

'You babble when you're nervous, don't you?' the stranger replied from behind the paper.

'Yes,' said Kevin biting his lip, trying not to babble. 'Who are you?'

'You can call me Pond. Jake Pond,' he said.

'JAMES BOND!' Kevin shrieked.

'No, Jake Pond!' the man said, making sure he pronounced the words properly.

'Oh, sorry,' Kevin said loudly. 'I still have some water in my ears. I'm Kevin.'

'I know who you are,' Jake Pond replied, pulling his newspaper down just a tad.

'How . . . how do you know?' Kevin was spooked.

'It's written on your cape,' Jake replied.

'Oh yeah . . .' Kevin said, looking over his shoulder at the bedraggled fabric. 'Anyway, I have to go. I'm not allowed to talk to strangers.' And he got up to leave.

'You're right, you shouldn't,' Jake said. 'But there's something you should know.' The man pulled the paper down from his face.

Kevin gasped. 'What!? I don't understand . . . we look exactly like each other!'

'I know. We have the same face, the same build; apart from the fact that I was born forty-five years ago, we could be twins. You couldn't make it up!'

'I'll say. I mean, you're tiny! How do you cope?'

'I'm happy.'

'You could be Grumpy, Sneezy, and Bashful too!' Kevin said in astonishment.

'No, I mean being small means you can creep around, blend in.'

'Are you sure we're not related, long-lost cousins or something? Do you have anyone in your family with three nipples? My dad has three nipples. It runs in the family. Tell me, do you have three nipples? THIS COULD BE IMPORTANT!'

'I don't. We're not related. I have no family. This is just a coincidence, an amazing coincidence. We're meant to achieve great things together. Kevin, I'm going to say something that may just blow your mind.' The man paused and looked around to make sure they couldn't be overheard before continuing. 'I'm a spy. I work as a secret agent. I used to love it, the travelling all over the world, the beautiful girls, the dental cover; it was amazing. There's only one downside.'

'What?' Kevin asked, his mouth open wide with astonishment.

'All the running around, the violence.'

'What about it?' Kevin asked eagerly. 'Oh, I see, that was the downside.'

'Have you ever found yourself thinking that you're meant to do something else, meant to *be* someone else?' Jake asked.

'Stop it, you're freaking me out. I was only thinking that today!'

'I can't take it any more, Kevin. I need to get away, just long enough to get my head straight. Do the simple things again. Being a school kid seems pretty easy. Maybe I'll try that for a while until I figure a few things out. Hey, I saw your little show in town earlier.'

'Oh no . . .' Kevin sighed.

'I saw you flying through the air. You were brave, fearless. I thought, that's a boy who wouldn't be fazed by the life of a secret agent.'

Kevin's face lit up. 'I do like to think of myself as an expert. I think I see where you're going with this. Are you proposing we . . .'

'Switch lives?' Jake suggested.

'Hmm, the old switcherooo.' Kevin smiled. 'I like it. You get to be a schoolboy, I get to be a secret agent for a bit.' He thought for a minute about the endless, fabulous possibilities. 'Yes, I can't see any disastrous and possibly hilarious mix-ups happening at all. As long as I—'

'Keep your head down.' Jake grinned back. 'You get to live in my apartment—it's full of gadgets to play with, there's a huge TV, and a takeaway pizza place round the corner, where I have an expense account. If anyone calls you, just say you're on a case and you need to go undercover for a while. You get to be a spy, without actually having to do any work! I get to go to school, play video games, do your homework for a week or three.'

'Do my homework!' Kevin squealed excitedly. 'BEST. DAY. EVER!'

Jake handed him the briefcase. 'In here are all the things you need: there's a false beard, some dark sunglasses, naturally, and the latest mobile phone technology.'

'WHAT?' Kevin gasped. 'A mobile phone! I'm so happy I could puke.' Kevin laughed, and opened the case for a look. 'When do I start?'

'You just did!' Jake smiled.

'Wait. What about our voices? They're different.'

'If anyone asks, just tell them you're practising for being an undercover school kid.'

'But what about—'

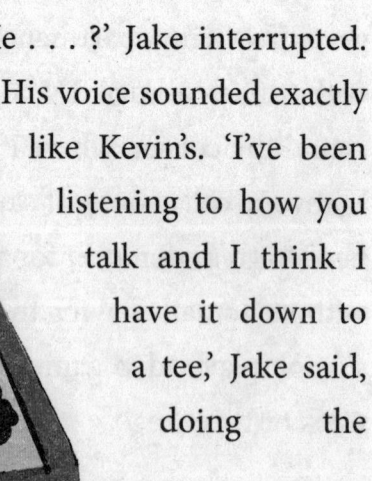

'Me . . . ?' Jake interrupted. His voice sounded exactly like Kevin's. 'I've been listening to how you talk and I think I have it down to a tee,' Jake said, doing the most perfect impression of Kevin that could ever be done.

'Oh my word! That's incredible! You're me! So is that it?' Kevin asked excitedly.

'I reckon so!' Jake said. 'The address to my apartment is in the briefcase, along with the keys. Just remember to keep your head down, Kevin. Don't let them talk you into taking another case and you'll be fine. Rest assured I'll keep my head down too. Give me your address and then we can swap clothes.'

'What? Here?' Kevin said, looking around him. 'Not sure naked in the park is a good idea!'

Five minutes later they had swapped. Kevin was in a suit, a dry warm suit, while Jake stood there in a cape and tights.

'Of all the days I could have found you, it had to be today,' Jake sighed, flicking his cape.

'Pretty cool, huh?' Kevin admired the costume— even Dad's pants.

'Yes, Kevin.' Jake stuck out a hand for Kevin to shake. 'We probably shouldn't be seen together. Just give me two or three weeks and I'll be back in the game. If you need me, I'll be at your place. Be careful.'

'OK,' Kevin said, giving Jake his hand. 'Good luck, Jake.' Turning away, he suddenly had a thought. 'Oh, actually, there's someone you should watch out for: Elle. She's my big sister, and she can be trouble at times.'

'Relax!' Jake said happily. 'I've fought some of the world's toughest agents, taken out some of the meanest villains. I think I can handle your big sister! Goodbye, Kevin. See you in a week or two and remember . . . !'

'Keep my head down and stay out of trouble!' Kevin said. 'I know. You can rely on me!'

WE ARE FAMILY

Kevin sauntered along the path. This was turning into a very interesting day. He'd fallen in love, gained a phone, become a spy, and it was only four thirty. It's a shame Jake told him that he should keep his head down and stay out of trouble. Kevin was pretty sure that he had the skills to beat up a few baddies of his own.

'Hiiiiiiiii-YAAAAAAA!' Kevin squawked, pulling off a few kung-fu moves he'd seen from YouTube as he went.

'Hiya to you too!' a voice came from behind a tree.

'Agggh! A talking tree!' Kevin yelled, terrified. Suddenly a head popped round from behind the trunk.

'Oh, phew!' Kevin sighed. 'I thought for one second trees had developed the power of speech.'

'Are you all right, 006 and a half?' The man lifted up his sunglasses and looked at Kevin closely. The man was well dressed, in a suit and black tie, and looked very important.

'I'm fine,' Kevin said, looking him up and down suspiciously.

'It's almost like you don't recognize me. Oh, I see what's going on here,' the man said, a look of realization crossing his features.

'You do?' Kevin gulped.

'You're undercover, aren't you, Jake? Trying out a new disguise? What a pro!'

'Yes, that's it!' Kevin breathed a sigh of relief. 'That's exactly it!'

'We need you to come into MI7, Jake. We have a mission for you,' the man said, his voice going

very serious the way grown-ups do when they have something important to tell you.

'Mission?' Kevin said nervously, remembering what the real Jake Pond had just told him. 'I'm good for missions, actually. Busy, you know. I've got something big brewing. It's a bit top secret, so I can't really tell you about it, but it just means I'm not able to do any actual new missions at the moment, I hope that's OK. I should probably go now. You know, go back to the apartment. MY apartment, where I totally live and get on with my homework, work at home, I mean, for the mission that I totally have got going on.' Kevin laughed casually.

'I'm not asking you, I'm telling you,' the man said. He pulled out a phone from his pocket. 'This is P. Bring the car round. We're taking Jake Pond into MI7. NOW!'

Kevin gulped.

Jake Pond carefully opened the front door to Kevin's house, took a deep breath, and yelled cheerfully, 'Hi, I'm home.'

Jake had broken into many places before, but this felt different. He wasn't sneaking around trying not to get caught; quite the opposite, in fact. For the plan to work, he needed everyone to know that he was there, that he was Kevin.

'Oh, hello, dear!' a voice came from the kitchen. Jake braced himself, put on his best smiling face, got ready with his best Kevin impression, and walked into the kitchen.

'Hi, Mum,' Jake said confidently.

The kitchen felt warm, and the air was full of delicious smells.

'Well, don't just stand there!' Kevin's mum said. 'Pass me the cheese, otherwise this cauliflower cheese is going to be . . . well, just a plate of cauliflower.'

Jake looked around and saw a huge lump of what could only be cheese. It was the most enormous piece he'd ever seen. Obviously cheese figured heavily in the lives of Kevin's family. Just a pity he was allergic.

'Oh, yummy, you know how I love cheese,' Jake said, trying to look happy.

'I know, darling. You *camembert* a meal without it!' Mum said, winking.

'Excellent cheese humour, Mother,' Jake said.

'Now go and tell your father that dinner is almost ready,' she said, throwing a lump into the cauliflower.

'Where is he?' Jake asked.

'The same place he always is; I'm surprised you had to ask. He's in the shed. I swear, if he could have popped a dress on that thing, he would have married it rather than me.'

Jake strolled into the living room of their little house and headed to the garden. He immediately felt at home; the whole place felt safe. Jake could clearly see that the garden was Kevin's dad's place, and it was immaculate. The lush green lawn looked as if it had been painted on, flowers growing tall and straight, as butterflies danced between them, feeding on their nectar.

'Hey, Dad, what're you doing?' Jake asked, peering in. The shed had a smell about it. A mixture of weedkiller and fertilizer with a whiff of cold metal from the various machines Kevin's father used to trim and tidy the lawn and borders.

'Plotting, son.'

'Plotting what?' Jake asked.

'Plotting how I'm going to overthrow the government and take over the world!!' Kevin's dad rubbed his hands together.

'Ugh!'

'Nah, only kidding. I'm just plotting where to plant this year's tulip bulbs. Had you for a minute, though!' Dad laughed and Jake joined in with relief.

'What's for supper?' Dad asked.

'Cauliflower cheese,' Jake replied.

'You Gouda be kidding me! I love cauliflower cheese!' Kevin's dad said, grinning.

What was it with this family and cheese? Did they own shares in cows or something?

Just then, Elle stormed into the shed. 'Dad, Kevin totally embarrassed me in assembly this morning, then totally embarrassed me after school with another one of his ridiculous stunt shows. Honestly, he's so embarrassing, Dad, could we not exchange him for a cat or something? At least make him go to a different school?'

'Darling, we've talked about this. He can't go to a different school. I'd appreciate it if you got that in your head. I still get emails from that place in outer Mongolia asking when Kevin is going to turn up for his first term,' Dad said sternly.

Elle just sniggered.

'Anyway, what do you mean, I embarrassed you this afternoon?' Jake asked.

'That stupid stunt show!' Elle barked.

'You mean where I did three perfect somersaults, before landing in the fountain?' Jake smiled smugly.

'No, I mean the show where you wore underpants outside your clothes, your trousers fell down, and you fell off the zip wire, spinning in the air before landing face first!' Elle snapped.

All Jake had seen was Kevin flying through the air like an acrobat! Apart from the uncanny physical similarity, that's what made Kevin perfect. He looked as though he could handle himself, like he was light on his feet, like he had the agility of a panther. *Perhaps*

Elle was just being a mean big sister? Jake decided to test the waters.

'That was all part of the plan!' Jake laughed casually. 'You know I've got the agility of a ninja, hey, Dad?' Jake said, looking for support from Kevin's father.

'You? Ha!' Dad exploded with laughter. 'Remember the one and only time we took you to karate? You had to stop because you got stomach cramps after five minutes, because you thought it would be ideal preparation to eat a burrito the size of a chair leg before the lesson. Two years later, and several buckets of disinfectant, and they still can't get the smell out of the community centre flooring. That's why we can never go back, son.'

Jake's stomach sank. What had he done? He'd turned a cheese-eating nerd into a spy for Her Majesty's Secret Service.

'You all right, son? You've gone awfully pale.'

Jake nodded, 'Yep, all good here. Completely fine!' Backing out of the shed, he added, 'Best go and do my homework before tea.'

'Do your homework?' Elle said, looking confused. 'You never do your homework. Just how hard did you hit your head? It's like you're a different person.' She was looking at Jake strangely.

Jake pushed past Elle, heading back to the house. He needed to calm down. *Maybe it will be all right?* he thought to himself. *All Kevin has to do is stay out of trouble.*

Yes, that was it. He needed a break and this opportunity was too good to miss. Everything would probably be fine . . .

5

FAST CAR

The car door swung open and Kevin climbed in. The interior was huge, dark, and cool. Kevin squeezed in between two burly men. Both were wearing sunglasses. Both had shaved heads that scraped the top of the car roof, such was the enormous size of their noggins.

'Hello,' Kevin offered. The two men said nothing. P sat down opposite Kevin and took off his dark glasses. Kevin could tell by the way the other two goons behaved that P was in charge and not to be messed with.

'You're a hard man to find, Jake. Thank goodness we fitted that tracking device to your briefcase. We wouldn't want you wandering around with the government's top secret secrets in your hands. The Chinese would give their eye teeth to know our nuclear missile codes and what the Prime Minister, Joe Perkins, has for breakfast.'

Kevin looked at the case and noticed a tiny light flashing on it. It would have been helpful if Jake had told him that *before* they'd swapped clothes.

'Oh well, you have it back. I'm done with it now. And I'm too busy doing other secret agent things, so you can give the job to someone else.' Kevin held the case out, his palms slick with nervous sweat.

'It's not that simple, 006 and a half. We need you; you're the best. We know you've been having some problems lately but we need someone prepared to die for the safety of our land. It's what you signed up for.'

'DIE? I'm too young to die! Think of the things I haven't done. I haven't grown

A BEARD, OR MANAGED TO ARMPIT-FART THE NATIONAL ANTHEM, OR BLOWN A BUBBLEGUM BUBBLE AS BIG AS MY OWN HEAD. I'VE SO MUCH TO GIVE!'

P looked at Kevin strangely.

'Oh, I see, you're staying in character, pretending to be a nerdy school kid. Tremendous acting and all that, old chap.'

P tapped on the partition glass and said to the driver, 'Take the shortcut: we have no time to lose.'

The car sped up and weaved through the back streets, eventually pulling up outside a grand-looking building. It was MI7 headquarters.

The car drove slowly through the gates, and Kevin couldn't help but gawp. He was starting to feel a bit out of his depth.

'So, did you see the game last night, lads?' Kevin said, trying to engage the burly men in what he hoped was 'blokey chat'. Kevin didn't know if there was a game on, but there usually was. Football, like the weather, seemed to be never-ending.

'Yeah, good goal, weren't it?' one of them said.

'I didn't know you were a United man?' the other said.

Oh no. Kevin had accidentally begun a conversation about football and he'd already used up all of his football knowledge.

'Oh yeah, I love the United. They are marvellous at all the kicking and the goaling. I love them so much that I often sing songs about them and hurt other people who support the ones who aren't the United team. That's how much of a United boy— erm—man I truly am. Hip hip hooray for the brave men of United, I say. After three . . . !'

The two henchmen looked at Kevin as though he was a maniac. Perhaps he'd misjudged his bloke chat badly. 'Or not . . .' Kevin sighed, looking at his feet.

'No time for that now, we're almost in,' P said.

Suddenly the floor began to sink and the car glided down into an underground tunnel. P opened the door and got out of the car. 'You two stay here. Pond, you're with me.'

P led Kevin down a long corridor to a steel door. A laser scanned P's retina and the door swished open. He led Kevin through a maze of corridors; each one seemed to have many rooms with some sort of top-secret work going on inside. Kevin craned his neck to see in through the windows. Maps were being studied, phone calls monitored, dictators being overthrown. In one, there were people being trained in martial arts, doing karate chops on blocks of wood. Kevin thought this was very unfair as no one had ever been attacked by a piece of wood.

Not on its own, anyway. He looked around nervously. *How on earth was he going to get out of this?* He promised Jake Pond that he wouldn't take on any missions. On the other hand, this was all very cool.

Finally they arrived in a big open room. It was full of high-tech computers and the odd bespectacled technician.

Kevin knew that he had to keep his cover at all costs. If they found out that he was a real schoolboy and not a secret agent, he would be in big trouble. All he had to do was keep his head down, and not take on any jobs. Definitely not take on any secret agent jobs.

Channelling everything he'd learned from Ninja Pizza Boy, Kevin decided to play along. Perhaps if he convinced them that he really was 006 and a half, he could convince them to let him go?

'Listen, Jake, we know you want out. We know you want to walk away from the job,' P said, looking sincere.

'Yep, P.'

'Yippee?' P replied.

'No, not "yippee", I said, "yep . . . P".'

'Oh . . .' said P.

'I have a dream, P. When all this madness is over, I want to live on a farm and raise chickens. Call me crazy, call me sentimental. But that's all I want. I've given this country all I have and now it's time to walk away,' Kevin said. 'So I'll probably just do that. Walk away, I mean. I've had a lovely time being a spy. But now I want to go, leave. I can't emphasize that enough.'

'I'm afraid that's not possible, 006 and a half. We have a job for you. One more job. Then you're done.'

'Can I say no?'

'No.'

'Why, P?'

'Wipeee what?'

'No, why . . . P, see?'

'There will be no "wipeee c", believe you me.'

'Who is Youme?'

'He's over there in the corner.'

Kevin looked round and a man waved at him.

'OK, OK, time out. Everyone, can we all stop

talking in letters? Let's use our words. Come on, we're the best this country has. It really shouldn't be this hard to have a conversation. To recap: I want to leave,' Kevin said, talking very slowly. 'I'm fairly sure you want me to stay?' Kevin said, gesturing at P. P nodded slowly. 'Words, we're using our words, aren't we?'

'Oops, sorry. Yes, I want you to stay. For one more job,' P said, speaking even more slowly.

'And I can't say no because . . . ?' Kevin asked.

'Because this is MI7, not the Boy Scouts, and if you don't stay and do this last job for us, I will hunt you down to whichever corner of the earth in which your tiny little body is hiding and terminate you using only a teaspoon,' P said with an icy smile.

'Well, that wasn't so hard, was it? We all know where we stand. Not entirely sure about your man-management skills there, P, but we'll come back to that another day. What's the job?' Kevin gulped.

P clicked a button on a desk and a giant computer screen popped up.

'We're after this guy,' he said, pointing to a picture of a middle-aged man in glasses. 'Dr

Brainiov is a computer genius, with a brain as big as an elephant's. He had been working for Mr Snelly for the past year, on something top secret and, more than likely, highly illegal. Mr Snelly is one of the greatest criminal masterminds at large but we've never managed to pin anything on him. His move to the UK from the US coincided with Brainiov's mysterious disappearance. We don't know why or how, but we know they were working on something big. We need to find out what Brainiov was working on before he went missing, and feel sure that Mr Snelly has something to do with his disappearance. Mr Snelly is one of the wealthiest men in the world so why would he choose to live in Croydon? We need evidence and we need it fast.'

'Hmm, good question. Croydon isn't exactly happening. Take it from someone who knows.' Kevin sighed.

'We need you to infiltrate Mr Snelly's house. His daughter is having a birthday party. We can get you an invitation and will obviously kit you out with the latest gadgets.'

'Gadgets?' Kevin said, his ears pricking up. 'What gadgets?'

'Tracking device, a TV watch so we can keep in touch . . .'

'Yes, yes, what else?' Kevin said eagerly.

'Smartphone technology, that goes without saying.'

'BOOM! AND HE'S BACK IN THE GAME!' Kevin yelled. He looked around the room and that's when he saw it. The phone he'd always wanted. 'The new MiPhone25!' he squealed. 'You have it!'

There was a geeky-looking technician programming it.

'The MiPhone25? Yes, it's only just come in. We have a special account with MApple. Well, the truth is, we've no idea how to get out of it; the terms and conditions are so complicated, not even our boffins know how to sign out. Still, it means we get all the latest gadgets here.'

'I don't care, it's all mine!' Kevin was so pleased, he even dribbled a bit.

'Sadly not,' the geeky assistant said.

'WHAT?!' Kevin screamed.

'A schoolboy can't have a phone that costs hundreds of pounds. It'll look out of place, you'll arouse suspicion. You need something a kid would have. Perhaps the Nokia Four,' P interrupted, handing Kevin a phone.

'My nan has this phone! It has big buttons so she can see them clearly,' Kevin yelled.

'Your nan?' P asked, slightly confused.

'If I had a nan, she has this one, would have this one . . . but I don't have a nan, because I'm very old and just pretending that I'm a schoolboy, obviously. Ahem,' Kevin said casually.

'Well, quite,' P replied.

Kevin examined the phone in dismay. 'Oh, good, I was afraid it might not be pink,' he said sarcastically. 'Or weigh as much as the moon.' Kevin was having second thoughts about this whole mission. What if he walked away and just went home and hid for a bit? *Yes*, he thought to himself. *He could get his old life back, get a haircut, a big perm or something, and*

would never, ever have to be a spy ever again.

'This is the party you'll be infiltrating.' P pressed another button and up popped a picture of a girl. No, not a girl, *THE* girl. The one he'd seen in town. He'd recognize her anywhere!

'I'll do it,' Kevin replied, immediately. 'I'll go now. I'll probably need some new clothes, to make me look cool, and some aftershave. Maybe some sunglasses and a hat—are hats trendy? Do girls like boys in hats? Would I look good in a hat? Help me, someone help me, I can't stop saying hats!'

'No, you need to keep up the pretence of the nerdy school kid, the one no one wants to talk to. The one who is so dull that he's practically invisible. Someone who can go to a party, not be noticed, and leave without being missed either.'

'You're quite the motivator, aren't you?' Kevin snarled. 'Fine! What are you going to dress me in? I mean, how bad can it be?'

6

IT'S MY PARTY

Kevin stared at himself in the mirror.

'You have to be kidding, right?' he said, shaking his head. He was wearing very small shorts with bright white knee-high socks, and a tight white shirt and bow tie. He looked like a ventriloquist's dummy, with most of the emphasis on the word dummy.

'It's perfect!' P said, smiling. 'You look odd enough so that no one will want to talk to you, but not odd enough to make anyone suspicious.

'We'll take you back to Croydon, then you can make your way to the party. We want you to infiltrate

Mr Snelly's office and find out anything you can about the whereabouts of Mr Brainiov. Remember, 006 and a half: blend in, be a ghost, float in, float around, and leave. Report to us tomorrow a.m. Got that?'

'Yes, go in, leave a round floater, and leave again,' Kevin said, trying to get his enormous phone in his pocket. 'Is there aftershave?'

'Good idea, every teenage boy uses aftershave. Put lots on—you'll really fit in,' P said, handing him a bottle.

Later that day, Kevin arrived outside the house. He looked at the invitation—this was definitely the right place, plus there was a huge sign outside which was a bit of a give away. It read:

PARTY HERE TONIGHT

'Thanks for the lift, lads,' Kevin said cheerfully to the driver and the same two henchmen from before. 'Hope the cough clears up,' Kevin added, thoughtfully.

'How much aftershave did you put on?' one of the henchmen said, coughing his lungs out.

'I wasn't sure how much to put on, so I only used half the bottle. Don't want to overdo it.'

Kevin got out of the car and walked up the huge driveway to the house. It was the biggest house he'd ever seen. Kevin worked out that he could probably fit three of his house in the footprint of Snelly Dwellings. They even had a security guard on the door, checking people's invitations. Above the door was a huge sign. It read:

ALESHA'S JUST BECAUSE PARTY

Kevin handed his invitation over. The man on the door looked at it, looked at him, looked at the card again, held his nose, and let Kevin in. Just at that second, his watch flickered into life.

'006 and a half, can you read me?'

Kevin looked down at his watch. Mr P appeared on the tiny screen.

'Hi, P,' Kevin whispered back.

'Who's happy?' P said.

'No, "Hi, P", I said, not happy. Do you not have a proper name I can call you by? This is getting confusing.'

'No, I'm P and that's the end of it. You've made it to the party. Let me know what you find.'

'Cool it, Daddio,' Kevin replied.

'What?' P sighed.

'I found some cool party phrases that cool people at cool parties say.'

'Really?' P asked. 'Listen, we don't have time for any of this now. I need you to go out to the back corridor—that's where we believe Snelly's office is. Find it, poke around, see what you can find.'

'I dig you,' Kevin replied. 'Over and out.'

Just then, there was a loud squeal from a microphone. Kevin stopped a passing butler and helped himself to a drink from the tray, then grabbed himself a mini-burger from another tray.

'Yum, these are great. Can you get me another tray or two, please? With extra cheese,' Kevin said. The room he found himself in was full of cool teenagers and their even cooler parents. They all hushed to let the rather large gentleman in the expensive suit talk.

'Hello, my name's Snelly. Thank you, thank you. I know a lot of people were surprised when we moved from our huge house in LA to this—'

'Tiny place!' a voice interrupted. It was Alesha! Kevin had been so busy concentrating on fitting in that he hadn't spotted her.

'Haha,' her dad laughed nervously. 'Our much more modest home, but it's about the people you surround yourself with, not the place. I grew up in this town, I even went to the local school, before I left and made tons of money. That's why I came back,

71

not to show off or anything, but because I wanted to give something back to the people here. I'm going to build a new factory, make new jobs, and give Alesha a different life experience. So that's why we thought we'd throw Alesha a party.'

'You know, just because,' Alesha said. Her voice was so posh her mouth barely moved—Kevin had never heard anyone talk like that before; it was as if she was royalty. Kevin was smitten.

'That's right . . .' her dad carried on, 'it's a "just because" party for my little princess. So raise your glasses to my beautiful girl, Alesha!'

'TO ALESHA!' everyone yelled. Alesha squirmed as if she was embarrassed, but everyone could see she loved everyone looking at her.

Kevin took his cue and began to weave through the crowds towards Mr Snelly's office. It seemed as though no one was taking any notice of him at all. They were too busy trying to work out what that bad smell was, although Kevin couldn't smell anything bad at all—just his rather excellent aftershave, Desperation for Men. The room was so big, it took Kevin a while to find the door. All he had to do now was slowly open it and creep through . . .

'Who are you?' snapped a voice. Alesha was standing in front of Kevin, looking at him in horror.

'The name's Twigg. Kevin Twigg,' Kevin said, in his bestest, coolest voice, which is to say not really cool at all.

'Twigg Kevin Twigg? What is that, German or something?'

"No, I mean, it's—'

'Why are you here? We'll come on to what you're dressed as in a second.'

'I'm here, just because . . . you know, it's a just because party . . .' Kevin smiled.

'Are you a clown? Why are you dressed like this? Are you a child clown, or are you ill? Your appearance and voice is making me feel unwell. I don't like clowns, they upset me. Father! Father!' Alesha yelled. 'Can you get rid of this clown? He stinks.'

'What do you mean I stink? You haven't even seen me juggle.'

'No, I mean you actually stink. That aftershave is pure desperation!' she said, before slapping him round the face.

Wow! She even knows the name of my aftershave! She is just amazing! Kevin thought to himself.

'But . . . but I didn't order any clowns, darling. I don't who this person is. Oh, my good grief, what is that smell?' Mr Snelly said. 'Oh, never mind. Security, get rid of this clown, and do it discreetly!'

Two burly security guards grabbed Kevin and pushed him into the corridor. The good news was that it was the one he'd been trying to get into—the bad news was that he was about to be hurled out of the back door. Suddenly Kevin caught sight of what must be Mr Snelly's office. Thinking on his feet, or what feet he had left as he was being manhandled down the corridor, he reached into his pocket and pulled out the bottle of aftershave. He waited until they were outside the office door then dropped it. The bottle smashed instantly, releasing a choking mist of fragrance. Kevin grabbed a hanky from his pocket and put it over his nose. The two security guards were temporarily blinded by the whiff and fell to the ground. Kevin crawled on his hands and knees into Snelly's office and shut the door. He jumped up and started frantically rummaging around, searching for anything that looked a bit suspicious. Kevin noticed that the computer screen was on and some files entitled 'Restricted Access' were being copied on to a USB memory stick.

'BOOM!' he whispered triumphantly under his breath.

Kevin watched as the last few files copied over

and then grabbed the USB stick and stuffed it into his pocket.

'Arrgh, my eyes. What was that, tear gas?' one of the security men moaned.

'Sorry, boys, it was my aftershave,' Kevin said, slipping back out into the corridor. 'I hope it wasn't too stinky.'

Both guards looked at each other and the next thing Kevin knew, he was being tossed through the double doors and outside. Fortunately, his face broke the fall. Feeling dazed and confused, Kevin rubbed his head and blinked wildly until his vision came back into focus. He felt in his pocket and grabbed the memory stick. Could this be the evidence MI7 were looking for?

7

MOVIN' ON UP

Kevin got up and dusted himself off. He felt tired but elated—he'd done it! He'd actually done something a spy would have done. I mean, admittedly, he didn't float in like a ghost, more reversed in like a bin lorry, but he'd got the result he'd been after. Kevin daydreamed about that evening's events as he walked through town. Particularly seeing Alesha. He stroked his cheek; it still felt hot where she'd thwacked him.

Kevin got to his front door and opened it. He climbed to the top of the stairs—boy, he couldn't wait to get out of these silly clothes. Kevin opened the door of his bedroom. It took about a second and half to remember that he didn't live there any more. Sitting on the floor, on his beanbag, playing his games console, was 006 and a half.

'You forgot that you don't live here, didn't you?' Jake Pond sighed.

'Ooh, yeah, maybe . . .' Kevin said.

'Shhh!' Jake hissed. 'You'll get our cover blown.'

'Oh, I'm sorry, I don't want to disturb your game-playing fun. I see you've made yourself quite at home.'

'This was what we agreed!' Jake yelled in the quietest way he could.

'I know, I know,' Kevin said. 'It's just a bit of a shock to see you using my things, that's all.'

'Tell me about it. What's going on with your family and cheese? You, sir, have a serious problem,' Jake said, looking at Kevin with accusing eyes.

'Hey, I could give up at any time, you know!' Kevin snapped back. 'Anyway, why am I defending myself to you?! You're the one with the odd life. I met your boss today. He threatened to kill me with a spoon. I'd much rather be here and playing Ninja Pizza Boy! Which, by the way, you're rubbish at. You can't even defeat the baddie at the end of level one. It's kids' stuff.'

'It's really hard to shoot him. He keeps moving around.'

'Here, try jumping and holding down fire . . . What am I doing? Why am I helping you? Wait, are those my pyjamas?! You've crossed a line, my friend. You never, ever, wear another brother's PJs!'

'Be quiet! If anyone hears us, we're both for it. Now listen, I hope you've been keeping your end of

the bargain and keeping out of trouble. I heard what *actually* happened in your stunt show. You told me that you were an expert at somersaults. Now I hear from Elle that the whole thing was an accident—you got tangled up and gravity did the rest.'

'I knew Elle would drop me in it,' Kevin huffed. 'You don't think I can do it, do you? You don't think I'm smart enough to be you for a couple of weeks.'

'I didn't say that, Kevin. Being a spy is hard. I mean, imagine if you had actually been called in on a job,' Jake chuckled.

'Hmm. Right,' Kevin said, looking at his feet.

'What? What does that noise mean?' Jake stared at Kevin.

'Nothing. I'm just, you know, doing as you said, staying out of trouble.'

'Good.'

'One thing, though. What if, what if, say I did, maybe, say yes to a job. I mean, what would happen then?'

'You'd say "ow",' Jake said, shaking his head in annoyance.

'Really? Why?'

Jake picked up a shoe and threw it at Kevin's head.

'OW!' Kevin squealed.

'I TOLD YOU NOT TO SAY YES TO ANY JOBS!'

'Well the boys at MI7 didn't give me much choice. They told me they'd hunt me down and kill me. Plus there was this girl . . .'

'Oh, for goodness' sake. You've been doing this job for one day and already there's a girl! How did you manage that?'

'Hey, don't hate the player, hate the game!' Kevin remarked in his own defence.

'What does that even mean?'

'I don't really know, but it sounded right.'

'What's the job?'

'I had to get some information on a criminal mastermind which I think I have done!' Kevin said, pulling out the memory stick with a grin.

'Good, at last some good news. Right, give it to me and I'll give it to P. I can take it from here,' Jake said, holding out his hand.

'No,' Kevin said sternly.

'What?'

'I said no. You don't think I can do it, but I can. There's not a thing you can do about it!' Kevin smiled.

'Seriously, Kevin, stop fooling around,' Jake said, inching his way to the door, to stop Kevin escaping.

'Oh, you think you can stop me?' Kevin said.

'Kevin . . .' Jake said nervously.

'I'm just sick and tired of no one believing in me,' Kevin sighed. 'Well, maybe it's time I started believing in myself. I work for MI7 now.' He puffed out his chest confidently.

'NO, YOU DON'T! I DO! I'm not going to be able to let you go out of this door,' Jake said.

'Door? Oh, Jake, you're so old-fashioned. Where I'm going, I don't need doors.'

And, with that, Kevin bolted towards the open window, doing a perfect somersault through the gap. Jake gasped in amazement for a brief second before grimacing in pain as he watched Kevin grab onto the drainpipe before sliding head first down it, and landing in a heap in the front garden outside.

'I totally meant to do that!' Kevin whimpered. Then he sat up and caught his breath, just in time for his trousers to land on his head. They'd snagged on the drainpipe. Kevin grabbed them angrily and walked off in a huff.

'Why am I always losing my trousers?' he complained. 'I'll see you in a few days, Jake. And don't worry, the country's in safe hands.'

'What's stopping me from going to MI7 myself?' Jake called out of the window.

'Because if you do, you'll be fired, probably put in jail. We're in too deep now, Jake.' Kevin pulled up his torn trousers and set off for Jake's flat.

'What a ridiculous person,' Jake said, shaking his head, watching Kevin sauntering up the road. 'The annoying thing is he's right. I'm just going to have to stay here and play one more game of Ninja Pizza Boy and wait for him to come to his senses.' He sighed.

Outside the bedroom door, in the dark shadow between the loo and airing cupboard, stood a figure. Someone had been listening the whole time.

'I knew you were up to something. I knew it . . .' came the demented cackling of an evil big sister. 'I have you now, Kevin . . .'

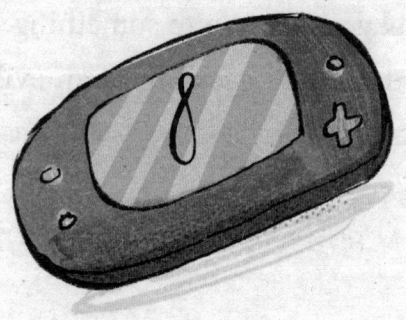

WHEN I GET HOME

Kevin stood outside the doors of an imposing tower block. It was in the part of town where the beautiful, rich people lived. The sort of place where you couldn't go ten feet without coming across an expensive coffee shop selling frothy milky drinks the size of a bucket. Kevin looked down at the key in his hand. 'Apartment 006 and a half . . . obviously.'

Kevin turned the key in the lock and walked through the grand hallway to the lift. The doors slid open—Kevin was so excited about the prospect of staying in a posh pad that he didn't see the shadowy figure sneak in behind him.

'WHAT APARTMENT, PLEASE?' came a robotic voice.

'ARRgh!' Kevin yelled, completely spooked. 'A talking lift.'

'DON'T BE ALARMED. I AM JUST A TALKING LIFT. I MEAN YOU NO HARM.'

'Errr, OK, apartment 006 and a half, please,' Kevin said.

'CERTAINLY, JAKE POND. WELCOME HOME. DID YOU HAVE A NICE VACATION?' the lift asked.

'Yes. It was lovely,' Kevin said, lowering his voice, trying to sound like Jake Pond.

'I'M HOPING TO GET AWAY MYSELF THIS YEAR. A WEEK OR TWO BY THE POOL WOULD BE NICE.'

'Well, yes. Wait, really?' Kevin asked.

'NO, I AM BEING WHAT YOU HUMANS CALL, "AMUSING". I'M A LIFT. I CAN'T GO ON HOLIDAY,' the robot voice chuckled.

'Well, yes, I did wonder. Excellent humour.' Kevin smiled nervously.

'I HAVE A BANTER CHIP INSERTED IN MY INTERFACE. YOU HAVE NOW ARRIVED AT YOUR APARTMENT. GOODNIGHT, JAKE POND.'

Kevin exited the lift and walked towards the apartment, but before he'd even got the keys to the lock, the door opened. As it did so, the lights all pinged on, a huge TV screen slid down from the ceiling, and a log fire immediately burst into life. It was like something out of the future! Kevin could get used to this! The walls were pristine white, the brightest Kevin had ever seen. The kitchen was fitted out in a silvery marble and the place was slick and minimal. Kevin spied a bank of buttons on the wall and pressed one. A computer voice came from somewhere.

'What mood music would you like?'

'Cripes, I dunno. Give me something funky,' he said.

Drums and guitars started playing; Kevin began to shake his hips.

Kevin pressed the next button along. Suddenly a huge siren started up and the TV, which had been showing some programme about cakes, started flashing red.

'MISSILE LAUNCH IN THIRTY SECONDS. SELECT TARGET, PLEASE.'

'Noooo way!' Kevin yelled.

'NORWAY SELECTED. LAUNCH IN TWENTY SECONDS.'

'GAAAAAAAH! Nooooo!' Kevin tried to make it stop by repeatedly hitting the button.

'GLASGOW SELECTED.'

'Massive idiot!'

'THE PRIME MINISTER SELECTED.'

'STOP IT, YOU STUPID MACHINE. I HATE YOU, I HATE YOU!' Kevin was now wildly jabbing every button on the panel in a complete panic.

'YOU HAVE SELECTED YOU. GOODBYE. LAUNCHING IN FIVE . . . FOUR . . .'

Kevin gave the button one last smack, and finally the countdown stopped with seconds to spare. Kevin made a promise to himself not to touch any more buttons. Without the siren, the apartment seemed really quiet, until . . .

. . . suddenly he heard a creak from the direction of the front door. He reached out to the side and, without looking, grabbed the first thing to hand. Doing a commando roll, Kevin dived across the kitchen to see a figure lurking by the door.

'DON'T MOVE OR I'LL SHOOT!' Kevin yelled.

'I'm not sure that banana's loaded. You're such a loser.'

Kevin looked down. The thing he had thought was a gun, well, it wasn't a gun.

'Elle!' Kevin gasped. He'd recognize her insults anywhere. 'What on earth are you doing here?'

'Wrong question. The question you need to be

asking is what are YOU doing here? Whose house is this, and why are you threatening people with fruit?'

'It's a long story,' Kevin sighed.

'I'm not in the mood for being messed about, I've just had to punch a sarcastic lift. Now you have exactly thirty seconds to come clean before I call Mum and Dad,' Elle snarled, pulling out her phone.

'No, NO! Please, it's really simple. There's this spy called Jake Pond, who looks like me. Anyway, he's having a bit of a bad time, so he wants a little holiday. He and I decided to swap lives, so he's now at home, pretending to be me. I'm here, pretending to be him. I also seem to be sort of accidentally doing a job for the government, who also think I'm a spy. I have to find out what's on this USB stick and then send the information to MI7. I'm looking for this guy called Dr Brainiov. He's been working for a criminal mastermind called Mr Snelly, but he's disappeared. So I had to go to this party, where this girl was and I think she fancies me, and I stole this USB stick and it's all a bit weird and please don't tell Mum and Dad. Please. Pretty please? Was that thirty seconds?'

'I don't believe a word of it . . . a girl fancies you?'

'That? That's the bit you don't believe?' Kevin shrieked, 'Did you not *hear* the rest of it?'

'Oh, I believe the rest of it.'

'Oh, really, why?'

'Because you're not smart enough to come up with something so far-fetched,' Elle said, raising her eyebrow.

'Thank you. Hang on, what?'

'Exactly. And I knew there was something weird about that other you. He did his homework and he left some of his cheese at dinner.' She looked around the stylish apartment and nodded approvingly. 'So you get to live here. For how long? God, this is so unfair.'

'Until I've cracked the case,' Kevin said proudly.

'No, seriously,' Elle replied.

'Why does everyone think I'll mess up?' Kevin opened the banana and munched gloomily.

'Have you not met YOU?' she snapped back. 'Still, nice pad.' Elle ran her finger across the wall.

'Just be careful, Elle, things aren't what they appear in here,' Kevin said, covering the buttons on the kitchen wall with his hand. 'I very nearly declared war on Norway trying to get the cartoon channel.'

'That's so typical of you,' Elle snorted.

'If you're going to hang around, you could try doing something useful. I need to find a laptop so I can see what's on this USB stick. There must be one in here somewhere. Help me look.'

'OK, but there will be a price. To find a laptop *and* for my silence.'

'What? What do you want?' asked Kevin.

'Hmmmm, yeah, I haven't decided yet. These things can't be rushed. I'm going to take my time and come to a proper decision. Do you know Mr Snipe, head of maths, by the way?'

'I'm not killing anyone. You can't ask for someone to be assassinated. No.'

'Oh, all right. You're such a goody-two-shoes!' Elle grumbled.

'Right, now let's find a laptop,' Kevin urged. They split up and started searching.

'What about this thing?' Elle said, pointing at the toaster.

'You know it's a toaster, right?' Kevin replied.

'You said things aren't what they seem,' Elle said in a huff, before pushing down the toaster lever. As soon as she did, knives launched from the slots in the top and embedded themselves into the ceiling.

'Will you be careful!' Kevin yelled.

'Aha! I was right,' Elle laughed.

'Yes, yes, OK. Let's just try to be careful from now on.'

'A laptop isn't likely to be in the kitchen. Let's try in the living room,' Elle suggested.

'Good plan,' Kevin agreed.

They dashed into the living room, and started riffling through drawers.

'HERE!' Elle yelled.

'Fantastic!' Kevin said. Within seconds he'd fired the laptop up and had the files from the USB stick open. 'I don't understand—what does all this mean?'

Kevin clicked on a file name called 'Dr Brainiov' and watched as numerous figures scrolled down the screen.

'It's money!' Elle breathed in awe. 'There's a pound sign and look at all those zeros! It looks as though there's a ton of money being regularly transferred to Dr Brainiov's account from somewhere called House of Cards.' Elle scratched her head. 'I know that place,' she said. 'It's the casino in town. I pass it on the way to the bus station.'

'Why would a casino be giving all this money to a computer scientist?' Kevin asked.

'Perhaps he won it at cards.'

'No one's that lucky. And why would Mr Snelly have this information? It looks as though massive payments are being made every month,' Kevin said. 'The casino is giving all of its money to a missing person. It makes no sense.'

Just then, Kevin's wristwatch started to buzz.

'It's P!' Kevin yelled.

'Who's P?' Elle asked.

'The boss man at MI7. If he sees you, I'm in real trouble.'

'All right, all right,' Elle said, slightly miffed.

'Hullo P! Good timing, I have something for you.'

'Always what I like to hear, Kevin,' P said from the flickering screen on Kevin's watch.

'I found a USB stick at Mr Snelly's house. It contains a file under Dr Brainiov's name and it shows loads and loads of money, I mean millions of pounds, going from a casino called House of Cards to Brainiov's account.'

'Excellent work, 006 and a half. All you need to do is infiltrate the casino, have a good old gander, and report back!'

'What! I thought you just wanted me to do this one job?' Kevin protested.

'Yes, this one job of solving the mystery. That's all.'

'Well you might have mentioned that!' Kevin sighed.

'Being an agent with many years' experience you

should know this, 006 and a half. Is everything all right?'

'Yes, of course,' Kevin muttered.

'Right, so I want you to go and see what you can find out at this casino. Why don't you come back to MI7 and we'll kit you out with a few toys? Get here as quickly as you can.'

Kevin's eyes twinkled. 'Toys, you say? Well, OK, if I must! Over and out.' P's image blinked away and the screen went blank.

'Boys are ridiculous,' Elle huffed.

'What?' Kevin asked. 'You'd better go back to our house, or we'll both be in trouble.'

'Oh, now the fun starts, I have to go,' Elle moaned.

'Thanks, sis. I owe you one.' Kevin smiled.

'You owe me more than one!' Elle insisted.

9

ACE OF SPADES

Kevin arrived at MI7 an hour later, strolled in through the main entrance, and was welcomed by P.

'Ah, 006 and a half, glad to see you're here. Good work with the memory stick. Now we really have to turn the screw, find out why this money is going to the missing doctor's account, and what the link is with the casino. But first we need to get you out of those clothes and into something way more appropriate. I think it's time for T.'

'Ooh, milk and eight sugars for me, please. Will

there be biscuits?' Kevin said, hopefully.

'Not that sort of T,' P said, shaking his head. '006 and a half, I hope you don't mind my saying this, but you seem different somehow . . . I can't put my finger on it.' P narrowed his eyes and looked at Kevin suspiciously.

'I'm just kidding! You know, being a really annoying kid.'

'Yeah, well, it's time to drop the act. You're off to a casino, and they don't allow kids in. Time to get back to the old Jake Pond.' P smiled encouragingly.

'OK, OK . . .' Kevin said, lowering his voice as best he could. 'I hear you, P.'

'You hear me pee? I'm horrified.'

'No, oh, never mind.'

'Let's go and find T.'

Two minutes later, Kevin and P were in one of the basement rooms of MI7. It was a mixture of underground bunker and laboratory. Clean and clinical, yet somehow menacing.

'You remember T?' asked P.

'But of course,' Kevin replied. He was getting

used to pretending to remember things he didn't have a clue about.

From what Kevin could tell, T seemed to be the chief gadget maker at MI7. Everywhere Kevin looked, there seemed to be another delight on offer.

'I see you've been busy, T,' Kevin said, looking around the room and picking up a pen.

'Please put that down!' she yelled.

Kevin put it back on the desk where he had found it. 'Why? Is it a missile launcher?'

'No, it was a present from my mother; she'll be furious if I lose it. This, on the other hand, is,' she said, carefully taking the apple that Kevin had just picked up out of his hand. 'Please don't eat that. We'll be mopping your brain off the ceiling for weeks.'

'Aha, the old exploding apple trick, huh? I like it, T,' Kevin said, trying to play it cool. 'And what does this button do?'

'Works the coffee machine.'

'Aha, the old coffee machine trick, huh?' Kevin smiled.

T looked slightly bemused. 'We have been working on a few new things. You see that piece of toast?' she said, pointing over to another desk.

'Yes?' Kevin said, looking at it.

'Pick it up and drop it.'

Kevin did as she asked.

'Wow, it landed butter-side up. That never happens.' Kevin was seriously impressed.

'Yep, that's right, we've come up with anti-gravity butter,' T said, with a self-satisfied smile.

'Cool,' Kevin said. 'And what would you use that for?'

'Well, to stop the floor getting buttery when I drop my toast,' T said, looking surprised.

'Oh, I see, not to kill a baddie, or catch a villain,' Kevin mused.

'You can't catch a villain with butter, 006 and a half,' P butted in.

'I see T, P.'

'Nonsense, there isn't a wigwam in the building!' P barked. 'Now stop being silly and let's get back to the mission.'

T pushed her glasses up to the top of her nose and nodded. 'Let's see what we can do.'

'Cool and the gang!' Kevin said confidently. 'I'm thinking lots of guns, obviously, maybe a bazooka up my sleeve. Not sure if that's possible, but you know, aim high, guys, aim high. And what about some sort of tiny helicopter? Nothing too complicated, you know, something that a child could fly, say . . . not that I'm a kid. Oh no, not me. I'm very old. I have a pension, and a shed, and a collection of beige cardigans.'

'Do you want to stop talking now?' T asked. 'You're behaving very strangely, 006 and a half.'

'Yes. Fine. OK. It's just been a long day. I'm not used to partying so late.' Kevin nodded.

'It's only eight-thirty!' said P.

'OK, Jake. First we need you to put on this suit,' T said, handing Kevin a smart pair of trousers, dinner jacket, bow tie, and crisp white shirt. 'The suit is made to measure, top spec Italian cloth, but it is also bulletproof. It's what's known as intelligent design. It protects you, even if you can't protect yourself.

There's something else too: the suit has an on-board computer with a "Wearable, Activated, Logistical, Lifesaving Intelligence" system installed, or WALLI for short. Say hello, WALLI.'

'Hello, 006 and a half,' Kevin's trousers said.

'Aargh! Talking trousers!' Kevin yelled.

'Please do not be alarmed, I am here to help,' Kevin's suit said in a robotic way.

'Sorry, it just came as a bit of a shock,' Kevin said apologetically to his own clothes.

'You're telling me! I used to be a sat-nav until last week, now I'm pair of trousers,' WALLI replied.

'Really?' Kevin asked, surprised.

'No, I am just doing the joking with you.' WALLI chuckled. 'I have been fitted with a ROFL chip.'

'Oh my,' Kevin said, shaking his head.

'Anyway,' T interrupted. 'The suit is voice-activated, and rocket shoes come with it, naturally. Lastly, you're going to need to do something about that baby face of yours—a moustache perhaps?'

'Ooh, yes, I've always wanted one of those! I mean, I could grow one at any time, obviously . . .' Kevin's voice tailed away. He did a little cough.

'Right.' T carried on without acknowledging Kevin. 'The suit also has a tracking device in it. The cufflinks have small detonators inside them, good for blowing your way out of rooms, getting into safes, that kind of thing. They can't bring down an elephant, or a kill a president.'

'Got you,' Kevin said, putting the suit on. 'Bring down an elephant, kill the president . . .' he muttered.

'NO! DO NOT DO THAT!' T and P yelled.

'That's not what I meant!' Kevin laughed it off.

'We will, of course, have the radio watch to talk to you, and there will be some money for you for any expenses. Will a thousand be enough?'

'A thousand what?' Kevin asked.

'Pounds,' P interjected.

'WHOOOOOOO! THAT'S WHAT I'M TALKING ABOUT. A THOUSAND BIG ONES.

I AM THE MAN!' Kevin slid on his knees across the room. 'I mean, yes, that should be fine.'

'Is everything OK, 006 and a half?' P asked.

'Me, what? Yes. All's well here.'

'I know that you need a break, and you'll have one soon, just try to hang in there and be less . . .'

'Less what?' Kevin asked.

'Weird? Could you try and be less weird?' P's smile looked less than sincere, considering it came with a look of concern.

'Less?'

'Yes. Be the opposite of weird, if you like. That'd be super!'

'Got it. I'm all over it, P. You can rely on me, T.'

'Meaty? Who's meaty?' T seemed perplexed.

'No, rely on me . . . T . . . honestly, you people and your funny initials. What's wrong with proper names, like Kevin?'

'Who's Kevin?' P enquired.

'Err, oops, no one. Just a normal name. Boring probably, in fact, let's forget I even mentioned him.

It's so boring and dull, I can't even remember it . . .'
Kevin spluttered.

'You said Kevin,' WALLI piped up.

'Be quiet!' Kevin yelled, smacking his trousers.

'Ow. What is this feeling of pain
I am getting?' WALLI complained.

'Right, it's time to go,' Kevin said, whacking
himself on the bottom again.

P and T stared on.

'Goodbye!' Kevin gave a cheery wave with his
free hand.

'STOP HITTING ME, MASTER!' WALLI
yelled in its loudest robotic voice.

T looked at P and P looked back at T as they
watched Kevin galloping out of the room, smacking
his own bottom as he went.

'Perhaps he does need a holiday after all,' P
sighed.

Fifteen minutes later, Kevin was standing outside the
House of Cards casino. He'd never been in a casino
but he sort of knew what they were—he knew you

could win money by playing cards or spinning one of those big spinny things, so if you spin the thing, and the ball lands on a thing, you win. Stop me if I'm getting too technical for you.

Kevin felt the wad of money in his pocket—it felt good. All he had to do was convince the people who owned the casino that he was in fact a very small adult with a huge moustache. Kevin twiddled his moustache—what's a moustache for if you can't twiddle it? P hadn't been sure about it, but Kevin liked the way it made him feel—like a cowboy in a dinner jacket, and it was time for a showdown.

Kevin opened the doors. Inside it was like a scene from a Hollywood party. Men in dinner suits and women in their best ballgowns were quaffing champagne and laughing in that terribly posh way people do when they drink champagne. Kevin wandered over to the bar. He climbed up on the bar stool and looked at the barman.

'Ribena, and make it a double,' Kevin ordered. *I'm excellent at blending in*, he thought, twiddling his big moustache. Kevin was excited, he had a feeling that the casino would somehow lead him to Dr Brainiov. He'd done so well to get that USB stick, this was going to be a breeze.

'Sure . . .' the barman replied. 'You look a little young to be in a casino, if you don't mind my saying, Mr . . . ?'

'The name's Mr Moustache . . . actually,' Kevin snapped back, in his best deep voice, thinking of the first name that came into his head. 'And yes, I do mind your saying. I'm pretty old, you know. I mean, does this look like the kind of moustache that you'd find on a kid?' Kevin asked, sensing he'd have to play it tough with the barman.

'No, I guess. Kinda an unusual name you've got there.'

'Moustache by name, moustache by nature. I'm just a moustache-loving guy trying to get some Ribena in this tough town. You got a problem with that, cowboy?' Kevin asked in his meanest voice.

'No,' the barman said, backing down.

'Good. Because do you know what happens when I get problems?'

'No?' The barman gulped.

'I'll tell you what happens,' Kevin said, really getting into the role. 'I crush them. I crush them with my fist and eat them. Then I poop them out and flush them away.'

'Cripes.' The barman seemed to be edging away slowly. Whether it was the threats, or the way his moustache waggled, Kevin couldn't say.

'So yeah, cripes is right. Now I'm looking for a guy, the boss of this place. Know where he might be?' Kevin snarled.

'He's walking the floor, sir, Mr Moustache, sir. He's the guy with the white suit,' the barman replied pointing him out.

'Good, good. This makes Mr Moustache very happy. There will be no crushing tonight. Only good times, my friend,' Kevin said, giving the barman a fistful of cash.

Kevin climbed down from the barstool and headed to the floor amongst the gambling tables.

There was the man in the white suit, right by the roulette wheel. Kevin sidled next to him to see if he could overhear a clue or some valuable piece of information.

'Would you like to place a bet, sir?' the man behind the roulette table asked.

'Err, what now?' Kevin mumbled, distracted. 'Yes, yes, I would. All on that one, please.' Kevin pointed, slapping all of his cash down.

There were gasps from everyone around the table.

'What, what did I do?' Kevin looked nervously around. He probably should have learned how to play before he started playing.

'No more bets, please!' the man spinning the wheel called. By now a crowd had gathered round. Everyone was watching to see where the ball would land.

'It'sss thirty-five black!' the man announced.

There was a huge cheer as everyone realized that Kevin had won. 'You've won half a million pounds, old boy!' one man shouted.

'Who, what, now?' Kevin smiled. 'HOW MUCH?! HALF A MILLION? YES! GET IN, YOU BEAUTTTTTTY!' Kevin started hugging everyone. 'I'm gonna get a phone. I can get loads of them. This is the best day ever!'

'Mr Moustache?' A voice came from behind him. It was the man in the white suit, the owner. 'Mr Moustache, perhaps if you stop moon-walking, I can get you your winnings.'

'Oh yes, OK. Sorry, folks, show's over.' The crowd started to disperse, grumbling a little. Kevin turned his attention to the casino owner. This was Kevin's chance to find out why so much money was going from the casino to Dr Brainiov's account. Kevin decided to pretend he was just another rich businessman. 'Drinks are on me!' he yelled. The whole casino cheered. 'BLAAAACKCURRANT SQUASH FOR EVERYONE!'

The crowd all sighed and tutted.

'I am the owner of the House of Cards. My name is Mr Miser.'

'Mr Miser, that's a funny name.'

'You're right, it certainly isn't as elegant as Mr Moustache, Mr Moustache. What's your first name?' Mr Miser enquired.

'Big,' Kevin answered without thinking.

'Your name is Big Moustache?' Mr Miser screwed his eyes up.

'I know. Mum and Dad were—how can I put this?—mental.' Kevin laughed nervously.

'Would you like your winnings in cash or cheque?' Mr Miser asked.

'CASH!' Kevin yelled, a little too enthusiastically.

The owner signalled and a man appeared with a huge suitcase full of money for Kevin. He opened it and handed it over.

'Come to Papa,' Kevin cooed, greeting it as if it were a long-lost relative. And then began to nibble and kiss the money.

'Erm . . .' Mr Miser said.

Kevin hadn't noticed that his false moustache was now stuck to one of the fifty pound notes.

'Err!'

'Will you stop saying that!' Kevin said irritably.

'Moustache.' The owner pointed at Kevin's face.

'Yes, that's me.'

'No, big moustache.' Mr Miser pointed at the pile of cash.

'Yes, well done, you've remembered my name!' Kevin said, grinning.

'No,' the casino owner said angrily. 'Your big moustache has fallen off. WHO ARE YOU?'

'Oh well, that's not important. I'll tell you another time. I'll go now.'

'Oh, you're not going anywhere. What are you? Ten years old?'

'I'm thirteen!' Kevin snapped. 'Plus twenty, because I'm a grown-up. Totally a grown-up.'

'Throw him out!' Mr Miser growled. 'And take the cash off him!'

'No! Not my lovely moolah!' Kevin yelled. But before he had time to grab a few notes, he was being hauled through the back doors, and thrown out into the trash by two quite massive men.

'Oh, man, so close! I had the money in my hand.'

Not only had he lost the cash, but he'd failed to make any headway with the case. 'Why do I always go too far?' Kevin muttered to himself. 'If I hadn't got distracted by that money, I could have done my job properly,' Kevin sniffed. *Maybe Jake was right; perhaps the life of a secret agent wasn't for him after all.*

Kevin's thoughts were interrupted when the two goons who had escorted him out appeared at the back door of the casino and into the alleyway. Kevin managed to dive behind the bins out of sight. This time the men were carrying something else. What was it? Kevin peered round a bin for a better view. The men were carrying out huge bags stuffed full of cash. Who does that?

'We need to take this to Big City Bank!' one yelled to the other.

Kevin looked at his watch. *It was late; what sort of bank would be open at this hour?*

'I hear good things about it; all the best gangsters bank there,' one thug said to the other.

'Oh, it's great, plus when you join you get a free piggybank and knuckleduster.'

There was only one thing to do: follow the money and hope it led to Dr Brainiov. Kevin needed to find a way to get into the bank without raising suspicion, and he had to admit that he hadn't done a great job of keeping a low profile at the casino. He couldn't turn to MI7 for help and all the real Jake Pond wanted to do was sit around playing video games all day. It was time for Kevin to face facts. He needed help and he knew just who to call. He needed the toughest of the tough. A person who was scared of no one. He needed his sister.

10

STAND AND DELIVER

'Say that again?' Elle asked, with alarm in her voice. 'Oh, it's perfectly simple, sis. I need your help to break into a bank and to bring down an evil villain.'

'WHAT?' Elle shouted down the phone.

'The money the casino is paying to Dr Brainiov's account is going through this Big City Bank—perhaps they have something to do with his disappearance? Why else would a bank be open at this hour? It's when the criminals come out to play. Will you help me?'

'OK, but you have to do something for me,' Elle said. 'My maths homework for a month.'

'Oh, all right, yes,' Kevin sighed.

'Then I'm in. I don't know why you have to make things so complicated.' Elle said, grinning.

'Listen, it's very important that you sneak out without Mum and Dad seeing you,' Kevin whispered into the phone as he perched on top of a wall next to the van. The goons had almost finished loading up the vehicle with money. He didn't have long before they'd be off.

'Oh, don't worry.' Elle reassured him. 'I'll be fine.'

'Really?' Kevin said. 'It's not easy being a spy, you know.'

'Don't worry, I'm not going to do something stupid like put on a false moustache and a funny voice, Kevin. I'm not an idiot.'

Kevin rubbed the top of his lip, where the sticky moustache had fallen off. 'Just be careful, that's all. I'll meet you at Big City Bank, in twenty minutes.'

'I'll use my bike; how are you getting there?' Elle asked.

'Good question. Let me worry about that.' Kevin hung up just as the last of the bags were being thrown into the van. There was no way round it: Kevin was going to have to jump. He waited for the two men to climb in the front and then leaped onto the roof rack. Kevin lay belly down, holding on as tightly as he could.

'Right, ready when you are, Mad Keith,' the man sitting in the passenger seat said, his voice drifting through the open window. Mad Keith popped on his hat and started the engine.

'Mad Keith—why do they call him that?' Kevin muttered under his breath.

The man in the driver's seat put the van into gear and pressed his foot to the floor. The tyres screeched in pain, as though they were a couple of scalded wild cats. The van seemed to go from still to warp factor ten in a heartbeat.

'THAT'S WHY THEY CALL HIM MAD KEITH!' Kevin screamed at the top of his lungs. 'OH, MY WORD, I THINK I'M GOING TO DIE. PLEASE HELP ME, SOMEONE!' Kevin wailed, as the van swerved and skidded its way through the empty streets.

'Can you hear something?' the passenger asked.

'Like what, Dave?'

'It sounded like the despairing scream of a tortured soul,' Dave replied.

'Probably just a loose wheel bearing.' Mad Keith fiddled with the stereo distractedly.

'OH, MY HECKY CRIKEY, WHERE IS THIS BANK?! WHY ARE WE NOT THERE YET?

PLEASE LET IT BE SOON. POOO IS GOING TO FLY OUT OF MY BOTTOM ANY SECOND NOW. WHAT IS GOING ON IN MY LIFE? WHY IS THIS HAPPENING TO ME? I HATE MY LIFE. I HATE IT!'

'Ah, we're here,' Dave said, at last.

Mad Keith slammed on the brakes and the van came to a sliding halt of burning rubber and diesel fumes.

'Did you hear that?' Dave said, tilting his head to the side.

'No, what was it?' Mad Keith asked.

'Ah, nothing. It sounded a bit like the relieved weeping of a small child who has just had a near-death experience. Probably the wind!' Dave laughed and climbed out of the van.

Kevin waited until both men had walked to the bank before he collapsed and fell off the roof. He slowly got to his feet and shakily began picking the bugs out of his teeth. Meanwhile, Mad Keith and Dave were at the door of the bank, punching in the passcode.

'Well, don't you look the bee's knees?' Elle said, sidling up to Kevin. 'In fact, I think you've still got a bit of bee's knee between your teeth.'

'I'VE HAD A VERY TIRING JOURNEY!' Kevin hissed, trying to keep his voice down.

'Quick! Hide!' Kevin grabbed Elle and they both crouched down behind a skip. Kevin put his hand over Elle's mouth to stop her making a sound. They watched in silence as the two heavies grabbed the bags full of money and carried them into the bank. Once they were safely in, Kevin let go of Elle.

'Owww,' she said sarcastically.

'Sorry, but I didn't want you to scream out.'

'I'm not an idiot, you know. I do get that we're on a secret mission. God, you're annoying,' Elle huffed. 'Can you please explain why you need me here?'

'I need you to do the distracting so I can get on with the important work of finding out about all this money,' Kevin said, grabbing her hands.

'Important work?' Elle sniffed.

'Sorry, I didn't mean important as in more important than your job. I just meant I need you to help me so I can find out what's going on,' Kevin said, apologetically. 'Now stop being weird and come here and pretend we're criminals, like a normal sister, while I stick on this oversized moustache.'

Kevin and Elle strolled towards the door and pressed the intercom.

'B*ZZZZZ*,' buzzed the buzzer.

'Yes?' came the stern response.

'Hello, I'd like to open an account, please,' Kevin said cheerfully.

'It's nearly midnight. We're closed.'

'Oh, really! How come you answered then?' Kevin said knowingly.

'I'm . . . erm . . . the cleaner. Yes, I'm cleaning. I'm just here cleaning the phone. That's what I'm doing.'

'Mr Miser recommended you,' Kevin said, winking at Elle.

'I don't know who Bob Miser is,' the man's voice came back.

'Oh, reeeaaally?' Kevin said smugly. 'How come you know his first name then?'

'Oh . . . errm, I clean for him. I'm his cleaner.'

'Oh, for goodness' sake,' Elle interrupted. 'Let us in. We're a couple of criminals looking for somewhere to stash some cash, you're a dodgy bank. Just let us in. It's freezing out here! It's not like we're the police or anything.'

Kevin shot her a look of fury.

'If that's true, and you do know Bob Miser, then you'll know the password,' the man from inside the bank replied.

'Well, we totally do!' Elle said knowingly.

'All right, what is it then?' the cleaner challenged.

'I'll tell you,' Elle said, looking at Kevin.

'Tell me then.'

'I will. Tell him, Kevin,' Elle said, nodding at Kevin.

'The password is—' Kevin thought quickly, '—"password"!'

The intercom buzzed and the door opened.

'How did you know?' Elle asked, open-mouthed.

'Everyone's password is always "password",' Kevin said, rolling his eyes. 'Now, just leave the talking to me,' he hissed.

Elle sighed loudly.

The inside of the bank was like no bank Kevin had ever seen. There were no cash machines, no pens on tiny chains, just a dark room with a shiny marble floor and scary-looking portraits of old, rich men adorning the walls. Kevin looked around but Mad Keith and Dave were nowhere to be seen. Kevin grabbed Elle's hand and they strolled towards the circular desk that sat in the middle of the marble floor. As they got closer, they could make out the man sitting behind the desk. He was looking very confused. Kevin discreetly made sure his moustache was stuck to his lip.

'Hello, can I help you?' the man behind the desk said. 'I'm Timothy. We spoke on the intercom.'

'Ah, the cleaner?' Kevin smiled.

'Yes, sorry about that.' Timothy spoke in a very

posh voice, as if he'd just smelt a funny smell. 'You can't be too careful in our line of work.'

'My name's Cecil,' Kevin replied, 'and this is my . . . er . . . wife, Ethel.'

'What?' Elle snapped.

'Sorry?' Timothy asked.

'I'm Ethel What. Yes, that's what I said, I'm Cecil's wife . . . apparently,' Elle said, looking horrified.

Kevin nodded indulgently. 'Haha, my darling. She's so funny.' Kevin chuckled awkwardly.

'You seem awfully young to be married,' Timothy said, looking very suspicious. 'Almost like you're children.' He narrowed his eyes.

'Would a child have a moustache?' Kevin twiddled his moustache, but not so hard it came off.

'Errr, no, I guess not. That's a fine moustache,' Timothy said, trying to lighten the mood.

'Thank you, I grew it myself,' Kevin said politely.

'Well, of course; how else would you get a moustache?' Timothy looked perplexed.

'Exactly!' Kevin nodded. He could feel Elle's eyes burning into him. She was going to make him pay.

She could barely stand being his real-life sister, let alone being his pretend wife.

'So, tell me, how do we open an account?' Kevin said, trying to change the subject.

'It's simple, really. A few details and we are at your service. Our bank vaults are the safest in town. We are very discreet. In our line of work we have to be.' Timothy winked.

'The bank vaults you say,' Kevin said. 'Could we take a look?'

'Yes, of course,' the banker said. 'I'll take you down there personally.'

Timothy led Kevin and Elle to the lift. Just as they got there, it pinged and the doors sprang open with Dave and Mad Keith inside.

'Eek!' Kevin yelled.

'Everything all right?' Timothy asked, turning round.

'My . . . er . . . shoelace—it's undone,' Kevin said, crouching down, desperate not to be spotted.

'Evenin' madam,' Mad Keith said, nodding as he walked past Elle. Kevin waited until the two goons were well clear of the lift and on their way to the exit before he stood up behind Timothy. The three of them stepped into the lift.

The doors closed and they stood in complete silence for a moment.

'You seem very young. I mean, to have such a distinguished moustache,' Timothy said, breaking the silence.

'Oh no, I'm quite old, you know. I just have an excellent beauty regime. Keeps me looking young!' Kevin grinned. Elle stared at her shoes.

'I can see,' Timothy said doubtfully. 'You could be no more than eleven,' he added, raising an eyebrow.

'Or thirteen,' Kevin suggested. 'Granted, I'm not the tallest of chaps, but I am, in fact, in my late forties.'

'Wow, really, I'm sorry,' Timothy replied. 'And you, Ms What, you look so very, very young too . . .'

'You do know it's rude to ask people about their age? Considering this is supposed to be the best bank in town for—ahem, shall we say—people like me, you're asking a lot of questions.

'Perhaps, dear,' she said, looking at Kevin, 'we should find somewhere else to keep our ill-gotten fortune?'

'Fortune?' Timothy's eyes lit up. 'No, quite, I mean, yes. I mean, fortune?'

The lift pinged again and they stepped out into the bank's vaults. Timothy got out first. Elle grabbed Kevin by the shoulder and mouthed, 'What are you doing?' at him.

Kevin shrugged and whispered back, 'I don't know! The whole wife thing just came out!'

'You're going to get us rumbled,' Elle muttered crossly.

'Once we're inside, I reckon I can hack into the computer and find out what's going on with Dr. Brainiov. You just need to distract Timothy.'

Timothy tapped numbers into the keypad in the wall and an imposing pair of metal doors creaked open. Inside was a huge room, with what looked like metal drawers on every wall, and a desk to one side with a computer and plant pot.

'These are our safety deposit boxes. They are the

safest in the world. No one has, or will ever, be able to get inside them. We have the best cyber-security too,' Timothy said, pointing at the computer. 'Can I ask what line of work you two are in?'

'Robbery, heists, the odd bit of kidnapping. You know, the usual,' Kevin replied.

'Yeah, the Great Train Robbery, that was us,' Elle added.

'Oh, really?' Timothy looked surprised.

'You know, the art theft, the one on the news last week? Yeah, that was us too. Basically, quite a lot of the bad stuff is down to me and him. Could you show me inside the safe? I want to make sure it's big enough. The *Mona Lisa* is not as small as everyone thinks.'

'But the *Mona Lisa* is in a museum in Paris,' Timothy said, scratching his head.

'For now . . .' Elle said, winking.

'Crikey!' Timothy gulped. 'Well, your collection will be perfectly safe here.' Timothy led Elle off into a side room, strewn with priceless works of art and other ill-gotten gains. 'This is where we keep all the most valuable pieces.'

'I'll stay here and make sure I'm happy with the safety deposit boxes,' Kevin called out.

Kevin waited until Elle had drawn Timothy into a detailed, complicated explanation of one of the paintings, then walked over to the computer. He removed a hat from the seat, sat down, and began to type.

'The cyber-security might stop anyone hacking into the bank, but it can't stop me from hacking from inside the bank.' There, in front of Kevin, was account after account.

'Aha! Dr Brainiov. At last!'

Meanwhile, outside in the cold night air, Mad Keith and Dave were getting back into their van.

'Cold tonight, innit, Mad Keith?' Dave remarked.

'Tell me about it. That's why I brought my . . . Where's my hat? Oh no, I've left it inside the bank. Back in a moment.'

Mad Keith strolled over to the front of the bank and punched the security code into the door keypad. The doors swung open.

'I just need a little longer,' Kevin mumbled to himself. He could see that there were huge amounts of money going into Brainiov's account, but the question was why? Aha! The casino was just a front. The real money—the serious dosh—was coming via the casino from a company called Sky Tech. Kevin quickly typed Sky Tech into Google. The head of Sky Tech was one Mr Snelly. That was weird!

'Everything all right in there?' Timothy called from the other room.

'YES. I JUST NEED A MINUTE OR TWO MORE TO ENJOY YOUR SAFETY DEPOSIT BOXES AND THEN I'LL BE HAPPY,' Kevin replied, knowing Elle would be able to hear him and would keep Timothy occupied a little bit longer.

OK, Sky Tech were paying money to Brainiov through a middle man, presumably so it couldn't get traced, but why? Why was Mr Snelly paying his missing employee all this money?

Kevin looked up just in time to see the lift had been called. Someone was coming. Kevin shut the computer down as quickly as he could. He noticed the hat which had been on the chair. He'd seen it somewhere before, but where . . . ? He picked it up for a closer look. Then it hit him.

'Oh no . . .'

11

SCHOOL DAY

The lift pinged open and there stood Mad Keith.

'YOU!' he yelled. 'How . . . why . . . and what are you doing with my hat?' He stared at Kevin, who was still holding the hat in his hand.

'What on earth?' Timothy spluttered, rushing in, closely followed by Elle. 'Mad Keith, what are you doing here? Do you know this man?'

'He's no man, he's just a kid in a false moustache!' Mad Keith screamed.

'How dare you!' Kevin protested, just as the

moustache fell from his face once again. Suddenly he remembered—he *did* have support!

'Activate trousers!' Kevin shouted, to the confusion of everyone else present.

'Please call me WALLI,' his trousers replied.

'Argh! That's so weird,' Kevin said. 'Can you hear me OK?'

'Yes, I am WALLI, "Wearable, Activated, Logistical, Lifesaving Intelligence"; or WALLI for short. Scanning surroundings to check for enemies. One moment, please. Beep. Beep.'

'We need to get out of here,' Kevin bellowed at his suit.

'Analysing the situation. Computing formula.'

'Hurry up!' Kevin said through gritted teeth.

'Did his clothes just talk to him?' Timothy said, aghast.

'WALLI has decided that the best

course of action is to use something precious as a bargaining tool. WALLI suggests you use the hat.'

'Nobody move, or . . . or the hat gets it!' Kevin threatened, for what he imagined was probably the first time in the world anywhere.

'You're holding a hat hostage?!' Timothy said in disbelief.

'DO AS HE SAYS,' Mad Keith piped up. 'IT WAS A GIFT FROM MY MUMMY.'

'Oh, I don't believe it. Please, oh, please don't shoot the hat—that would be really terrible. Oh, what a senseless waste of an accessory,' Timothy cried mockingly.

'Everyone be quiet. Here's what we're going to do—' Kevin started.

THWACK!

Elle smashed Timothy over the head with a priceless Van Gogh painting which she had grabbed from the safe. When he was down, she did the same to Mad Keith with a gold bar.

'Or hit them over the head. Yes, you could also do that,' WALLI said.

'What did you do that for?' Kevin screamed.

'I was helping you!' Elle shouted.

'I had it all under control; you could have killed them both! Plus you've destroyed a priceless work of art.'

'He's not dead!' Elle shouted. 'Is he?' She checked Timothy and Mad Keith's pulses. 'They are totally not dead. Now stop moaning. I saved your life!'

'When they wake up, they're going to be after us big time. You've just made everything ten times worse!' Kevin yelled.

'Oh, really, what were you going to do with that

hat? Kidnap it and hold it to ransom, you ridiculous human being?'

'I knew I should never have asked for your help. You've done nothing except get in the way!' Kevin shrieked.

'You'd still be outside if it wasn't for me!' Elle shouted. 'There's a Rembrandt out there that is ready for smashing if you want to go down *that* road, you little twerp.'

'Ugghhhhh,' Timothy moaned.

'Quick, he's waking up!' Elle shrieked. 'Do you have everything you need?'

'YES!' Kevin snapped back.

'Uggh . . .' Timothy groaned. 'What happened?'

'You fell,' Kevin said, looking concerned. 'You hit your head on a masterpiece of post-impressionist Europe.'

Everyone looked at Kevin.

'What? I read books.' Kevin shrugged.

'You hit me!' Timothy grimaced in pain. Just at that moment Mad Keith began to stir too.

'Shall we go?' Elle asked urgently.

'Yeah, that's probably a good idea.'

Elle and Kevin ran towards the lift and pressed the button. Timothy staggered to his feet and looked at the computer screen.

'You two!' he yelled after them. 'Who are you?'

The lift pinged open and Elle and Kevin rushed in before hitting the button as hard as possible. Timothy ran towards the open doors but they slammed shut a second before he got there. The lift zoomed back to the foyer, where Kevin and Elle hurried out through the front door and into the street.

'Never, EVER ask me for a favour again!' Elle bellowed at Kevin. 'You are the biggest loser I've ever met. You could have got us killed!'

'ME?' Kevin yelled back incredulously.

'Yes, you. You'd better come home with me before you get yourself into any more trouble. We can make that Jake Pond guy swap back and everything can go back to normal.'

'Don't you understand, Elle? I don't want things to go back to normal, stuck in a dead-end town with a horrible bully for a big sister,' Kevin sneered. Just then, Timothy skidded after them on to the street.

Elle jumped on her bike. 'Come on, Kevin, get on!'

'No.'

As Timothy gained on them, Kevin ran in the opposite direction to Elle, towards Jake's apartment, his eyes stinging with tears. Elle watched him go and screamed in frustration, but as Timothy approached, Elle had no choice but to speed off towards home.

Kevin woke with a start. For a split second, he'd forgotten where he was. He'd forgotten about last night; he'd forgotten that he was an accidental secret agent. Then it hit him. He felt his blood run cold and his chest felt heavy. He ran through his argument with Elle from the night before. *Maybe he should just go home and forget about this stupid job?* Kevin rubbed the sleep from his eyes and got out of bed. He gazed out onto the river and thought about his old life, his friends, his mum and dad, his stupid sister. He suddenly felt very alone. He wished he could just click his fingers and make it all go away, but he was in too deep now; he knew too much. There was only one way to get his old life back and that was to complete the job. He cared about what happened to Dr Brainiov and whatever Mr Snelly was up to; Kevin had a responsibility to stop it. Nothing made sense, but the only thing Kevin knew was that he was stuck in the middle of all this, and he was going to stay stuck unless he could solve the case.

Kevin went to the bathroom to brush his teeth. He looked at himself in the mirror and it was like looking at himself for the first time. He had to make everything right and there was only one person that could give him the advice he needed—the real 006 and a half.

Kevin hopped off the bus and headed back towards his school, taking the back streets in case he was recognized. At the school gates, Kevin crouched down and looked out—the coast was clear. Kevin took a deep breath and scurried in. He'd only been away from school for a few days but it felt like a lifetime ago. Kevin looked at his watch; it was nearly ten o'clock. That meant 006 and a half should be in English. Kevin sneaked to the door and took a peek inside. He was breathing so loudly that he was sure someone would hear. The class were all staring at the front in silence. What were they looking at? Kevin opened the door a fraction and craned his neck. It was 006 and a half!

'Now come on, Kevin,' his teacher, Mrs Frink, said. 'We've all had to do it. Now it's your turn.'

Suddenly Kevin remembered. Today was the day he was supposed to read out his poetry assignment in front of the whole class. He reckoned he probably should have mentioned that to Jake at some point.

'But I don't want to,' Jake Pond said, his expression steely and determined.

'I know you don't want to, that's the point. We're here to express our feelings. That's what poetry is about: feelings.'

'Feelings are bad. They are a sign of weakness. If your enemy knows your weakness, they will kill you.'

'No one's going to kill you, Kevin, for sharing some poetry. I might kill you if you don't share, though,' Mrs Frink sighed.

'I doubt it, I'd snap you like a twig,' Jake muttered under his breath.

'Oh, just get on with it, boy!' she yelled, finally losing her patience.

'Fine,' Jake huffed. He took a deep breath and started . . .

'I am here, I am here right now.
Being a poet.
Words coming out of my face, like a . . .
*   waterfall of letters.*
Talking about feelings . . .
Not potato peelings.
Dreaming . . .
of being free from this feeling
of seeing my feelings
peel like a scheming
leaning, tree. Swaying in the wind
in a forest of bleakness,
this is my weakness
that I hope they see.

The real me . . . free.
Happy in my misery
as I share with you my poetry . . .
. . . with thee.'

006 and a half stood in silence. Mrs Frink suddenly began to dab her eyes. 'Oh, Kevin, that was magnificent.'

'I know,' he said. 'Can I sit down now?'

The rest of the class burst into applause, their mouths open wide in amazement. Kevin could see Stu and Peter looking at each other at the back of the class; they looked confused as if they knew something was amiss.

'A forest of bleakness . . . ?' Kevin muttered from behind the door, shaking his head.

'I'm putting you forward for the school talent show at the end of the month. Will you do some more in front of the whole school?' Mrs Frink smiled excitedly. 006's shoulders sank but he nodded politely.

'Class dismissed!' The teacher could barely be heard over the bell and the scraping of chairs as the class prepared to escape.

Kevin scarpered behind the coat pegs and waited for the class to file out. 006 and a half was last to leave.

'Hey, I didn't know you wrote poetry so well?' Pete yelled at Kevin.

'Yeah, it was weird, like it was a different you,' Stu agreed.

'Well, I've been working on it in private. I didn't want anyone to know.' 006 and a half smiled nervously.

'Pssssst!' Kevin hissed loudly from behind the coats.

'I'll catch you guys up. I just need to go to the bathroom,' 006 and a half said, patting the lads on the shoulders.

'OK,' Stu replied, as they carried on up the corridor.

Jake Pond stopped in his tracks. He turned round and peered behind the coats. 'What are you doing here? If anyone sees you, our cover will be blown.'

'I know, I was careful. I don't know what to do, Jake. I'm not sure I'm up to this. Everything is such a mess.'

'Why, what's happened?' Jake asked, hiding amongst the coats with Kevin.

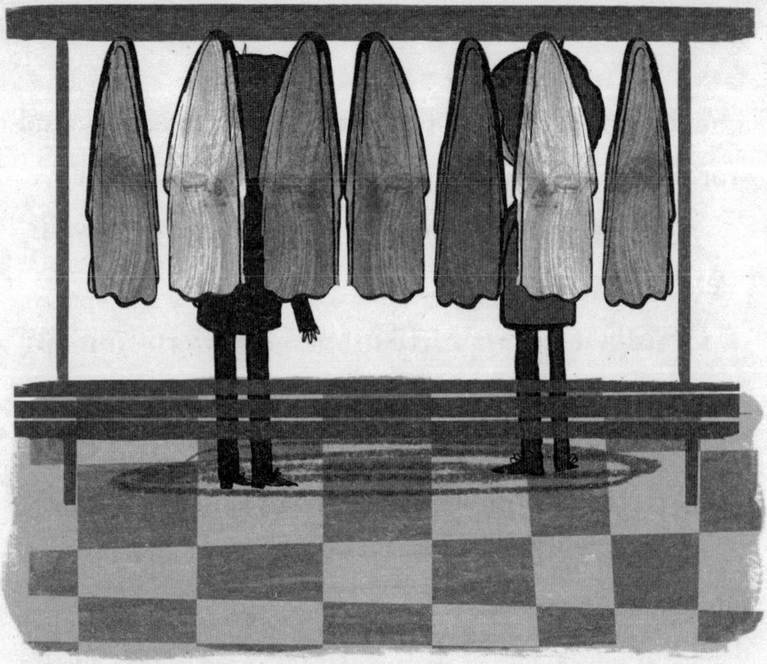

'A computer genius called Dr Brainiov was working on something big with this millionaire, Mr Snelly, who's just moved back to town. Brainiov went missing but Snelly is still putting a lot of money into Dr Brainiov's bank account via a company called Sky Tech. Something weird is definitely going on. And then I had a big row with my sister and now everything is terrible. I'm useless.'

'Wait, you found all this out?' Jake said, startled.

'Oh, it wasn't that hard. I managed to infiltrate a casino and break into a bank. I'm sure you would have done it so much better than me, but there you go!' Kevin sighed.

'No,' Jake replied.

'No, what?' Kevin asked.

'No, I couldn't have done it better. You did brilliantly.' Jake looked impressed.

'Look, you don't have to make fun of me, I know I'm a big loser. You can have your old life back, and I'll have mine. You were right, I was wrong!'

'No, I was wrong,' Jake said. 'I'm not making fun of you. You sound like you've almost cracked the case.'

'Are you serious?' Kevin asked.

'Yes!' Jake nodded enthusiastically. 'You need to finish the job. Investigate Sky Tech—that's the key to all this. But you probably knew that already, didn't you? Besides, I'm really starting to enjoy this poetry malarkey. Great therapy; I haven't felt like killing anyone in literally days.'

'What? Really, you think? Wow. I mean I guess you either have it or you don't. Some people are the real deal, like you and me, Jake Pond; others are just, well, the opposite of the real deal . . . you know.'

'Stop talking.'

'Yes.'

'Here's what you need to do: break in to Sky Tech, try and tie it all together with Snelly, and find Brainiov. Just keep going and try to talk less.'

Kevin nodded, took a breath, opened his mouth, closed it again.

'Oh, for goodness' sake, you can talk now!' Jake Pond sighed.

'Great. Listen, this is all tremendous advice, but how?'

'Use everything that MI7 gave you—it'll make things easier. Now I need *your* help. This place is weird. Everyone talks in a strange language, people are always ROFL-ing, and everyone has strange haircuts. There's a girl in English class who keeps sending me silly notes, with hearts written on. HELP ME!'

'Take her out,' Kevin said helpfully.

'Have her exterminated. Hmm, seems extreme, but OK.'

'No! I mean, you know, to the cafeteria. Buy her a

milkshake and tell her you just want to be friends . . . wait a second. What do you mean they're sending *you* love hearts? They're sending them to me—they think you're *me*. You're stealing my girlfriends!'

'She just sent me one saying my poetry moved her. I can't help it if I'm a natural!'

'What, the potato poem? Blimey, some people have no taste!'

'Hey, my teacher thought it was good. So good I have to do more in front of the whole school!' Jake grinned triumphantly.

Kevin stared at him with his eyebrow raised.

'Oh no, I have to do another poem in front of the whole school . . .' Jake Pond had a look of dread on his face as realization dawned.

'There it is. Yes, you do. Well, enjoy it, poetry boy. I have to go and save the world!'

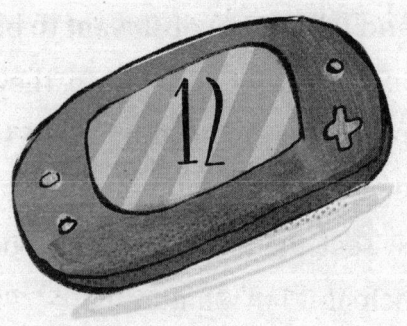

JUMP AROUND

Kevin was back in his MI7 suit and standing outside a dilapidated building on an industrial estate with a sign which read 'Sky Tech' on the wall and gigantic forbidding gates.

'Rightio,' Kevin said. Kevin always said 'Rightio' when there was anything strenuous to be done, like understanding algebra or getting out of a chair after a particularly big lump of cheese. He took a step back and ran towards the metal gate with all his might. It occurred to him a couple of seconds into his run-up that he wasn't entirely sure what he was going to do when he got to the gates. Was his plan to burst through them, leaving a rather large Kevin-shaped hole in the middle, or was he going to break them open like a charging rhino? Neither seemed particularly likely to be successful. Perhaps if he said the name of a dead Native American warrior just before he hit them, that would help.

'GERONIMOOOOOOOO!' Kevin yelled. What Kevin had failed to realize was that the gates were unlocked. There was a brief moment of triumph as he broke through, followed by waves of panic as he realized he couldn't stop running in time and was about to hit the . . .

'Arrrrrgh, bloomin' wall!' Kevin wailed.

When he had recovered, Kevin looked around. The place seemed deserted but how was he going to break in?

'Errr, excuse me, WALLI.'

'Do you need help with anything?' came the robotic response.

'Yes, WALLI, I do. I need to get into this building here, please. Where's best?' Kevin asked his trousers.

'That would be that top floor window up there.'

Suddenly Kevin's arm shot up and pointed at a window at the very top of the building.

'Arrgh, you made my arm move! P never said you could do anything like that!'

'Yes. I am WALLI. It stands for . . .'

'Yes, I know. OK, how do we get up there?' Kevin asked, looking up at it. 'It must be a hundred feet.'

'We jump,' WALLI answered.

'Jumppppppppppppppppparrrrrrrgh!'

Kevin screamed as he hurtled through the air with the speed and grace of a bowl of jelly being fired out of a cannon. Rocket jetpacks had emerged from the bottom of his shoes, and he burst through the window, showering glass everywhere.

'Oh my, no, help me! I'm going to break every bone in my body.'

'Automatic landing system deployed,' WALLI calmly replied.

At that second, large springs uncoiled from his soles and Kevin came to a boinging landing.

'Next time you do that, WALLI, could you at least warn me? I nearly wet myself.'

`Please do not do wee-wees in your pants, master. That will compromise my system and I will be forced to electrically displace my battery and short-circuit myself.'

'Oh, great. You mean, if I get wet, my trousers will explode?' Kevin sighed, dusting the broken glass out of his hair.

`Affirmative,' WALLI calmly replied.

'Well, excellent safety tip. Well done all round.' Kevin gasped. 'Wait, can you hear a pathetic whimpering sound?'

`Affirmative,' WALLI replied. `I assumed it was you.'

'You know, you're a real hoot to have around, WALLI.'

`I know, master. I am running lolz 2.0.'

'The name's Kevin, but master will do.'

`I thought your name was 006 and a half?'

'Errr, 006 and a half is short for … errm … Kevin.'

`Really, I thought . . .'

'Look,' Kevin said impatiently, 'I don't have time for this. I can hear something—let's go and investigate.'

`Yes, 006 and a half, let me calibrate where it's coming from. Deploying radar.'

Without warning, Kevin's arms shot out and his hands cupped his ears. `Can you hear anything?' WALLI asked.

'Oh, great radar system you have there, using my ears.' Kevin listened closely. 'I think it's coming from in that room over there.'

Kevin boinged over to a dust-covered door and gave it a gentle push. It creaked open and, there inside, handcuffed to a chair, with a gag in his mouth, was a man.

'Grooooou muuuuuuspt hullllp meeeeee, I'gmmm Droctror Braiiiiigniofffs!'

Kevin rushed over to Dr Brainiov and pulled the rag out of his mouth.

'You have to help me,' he spluttered, 'the world is in great danger.'

13

DOCTOR DOCTOR

'Who did this to you?' Kevin asked.

'Mr Snelly. He forced me to keep working for him even after I found out his evil plans,' the doctor sighed.

'Please tell us all you know, from the beginning.'

'Did your trousers just say something . . . ?' Dr Brainiov said, his nose wrinkled with confusion.

'Yes. Don't mind them, they're on our side.' Kevin smiled reassuringly.

'Yes, but talking trousers? That's a bit weird, isn't it?' Dr Brainiov asked.

'I can hear, you know. I do have ears,' WALLI grumbled, 'and feelings . . .'

'No, you don't!' Kevin snapped.

'No, fair enough, you got me there. I don't have feelings, but I do have ears. In fact, if you pull my pockets out, I'll be able to hear better.'

'Oh really, must we? I already have springs on my shoes, and now I have to pull out my pockets too?' Kevin complained.

'Yes, please, master.'

'Is anyone else hearing and seeing this, or have I gone mad?' Dr Brainiov whimpered.

'Dr Brainiov, please calm down. It's just a robotic suit, there's nothing to be scared of. Now from the beginning, tell me what happened.' Kevin pulled out his pockets and sat down on a nearby chair.

'I was Mr Snelly's chief engineer—he had the ideas and I designed them. I thought we were a team. Things changed when Snelly started to work for someone else. I never met him but Snelly called him 'sir', as though he were still at school. Snelly asked me to come up with a computer virus that would mutate and change over time so it couldn't be stopped. Like a real virus. I refused so he kidnapped me. He said unless I did what he told me, he'd chop me and my family up into little pieces and feed them to a bear.'

'Sounds grizzly,' Kevin replied. 'But how is the world in great danger?'

'He's planning to destroy the internet.'

'Destroy the internet?' Kevin gasped. 'Can that be done?'

'It's like destroying anything, just because it exists in computers doesn't mean it can't be broken. This virus will shatter the internet into a billion pieces.'

'How do we know you're not in on this evil plan? What about all the money flowing into your account from Sky Tech?'

'Sky Tech is a front—it doesn't really exist. The money is from Snelly's criminal activity and it's all been sunk into building this virus. Oh, what have I done?'

'You had no choice,' Kevin said reassuringly.

'Maybe the world would be better off without the internet?'

'The world wouldn't work without the internet! It's not just funny cat videos; it's the way we communicate with each other, from governments, to business, to banks, to *everyone*. Snelly could destroy the world as we know it!'

'Crikey,' Kevin said, gulping.

'Crikey, indeed. But how did you find me? You're just a kid!'

'I work for MI7. We've been watching Snelly for some time and then when we heard you were missing I followed the trail.'

'Snelly's been pretending Sky Tech's real, putting distance between him and his plan. So that if anything went wrong, he could blame it all on me, say that I was a mad scientist and that I had been using his money to carry out *my* dastardly plan. But I had nothing to do with it! Snelly has the virus on a data chip; he just needs to upload it, open a link, and it will spread to every computer in the world before you know it,' Dr Brainiov said sadly.

'Let's get you out of here and go after Snelly. Where are the keys to the handcuffs?' Kevin said, looking around.

'On the desk in the back room.' Brainiov answered, gesturing with his head.

Kevin opened the door to a room containing dozens of computers. This was obviously the place where Snelly made Brainiov do all his dastardly work.

'Which desk? There are loads,' Kevin said, trying to spot the key.

'The one with bomb on it,' Dr Brainiov replied.

Kevin froze. He stared back at the doctor, then again into the room. Sure enough, there was a desk to his left with a computer, a small set of keys, and what looked like a huge bomb.

'Bomb?' Kevin said, trying to sound nonchalant.

'Yes, Snelly is going to blow this whole place up. He'll be here any minute.'

Kevin looked at his trousers. 'ARRRRRRRRRRGH!!!!!' Kevin and his trousers both cried.

'WALLI, if Snelly is on his way back here to blow the place up then it's likely that he has the virus with

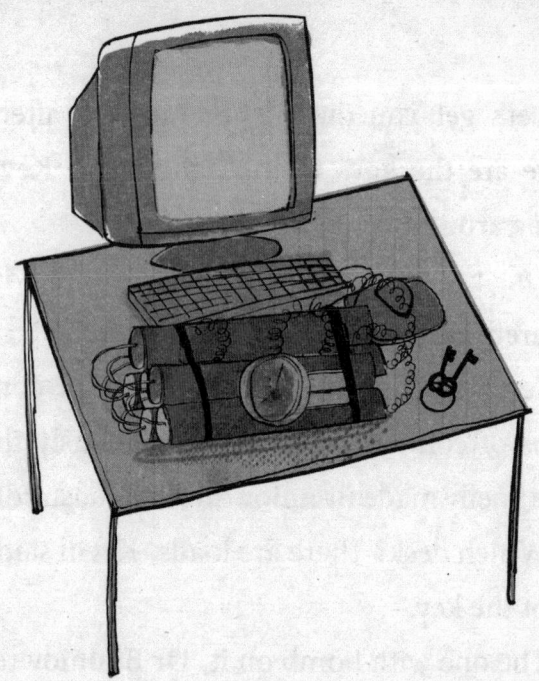

him too. All we need to do is to destroy the virus and stop Snelly blowing us all up. We need backup! My watch isn't working.'

'I'm trying to call MI7 but I can't get a signal. It must be something to do with all these computers causing interference. I might be able to send a text message to a phone,' WALLI said.

'Yes, do that. Find one of my contacts—anyone— and tell them we need help.'

Elle was walking home from school in a stinker of a mood. Her phone beeped in her school bag. She didn't even bother to look at it. She was so annoyed with Kevin for all the stupid things he'd done—for running off like that after the bank break-in. Although, perhaps she shouldn't have been so harsh. And maybe he wasn't a *total* loser . . . Elle's tummy lurched. Why did she feel bad? Could it be—Elle struggled to even think it, let alone say it out loud—that Kevin *wasn't* an idiot? Elle wrestled with the idea that maybe she was a little bit proud of him, perhaps even a little jealous that he was good at something. Her phone beeped again.

'Oh, who is this and what do they want?' she snapped. But her expression changed as soon as she read the message.

14

BOOM, BOOM, SHAKE THE ROOM

'GIVE ME A FEW MINUTES AND WE'LL BE DONE!' yelled Mr Snelly to Alesha as he piloted his helicopter over the city. 'I'VE GOT ONE LAST PIECE OF BUSINESS TO TAKE CARE OF!'

Alesha rolled her eyes. Rolling her eyes was one of Alesha's favourite things to do. She found that it displayed the maximum emotion she was feeling, with the least amount of effort.

'Whatevah,' Alesha muttered.

'I KNOW, IT'S BEAUTIFUL WEATHER, ISN'T IT? I'M SO GLAD THAT YOU CAME WITH

ME . . . IT'S GOOD TO SPEND SOME FATHER-
AND-DAUGHTER TIME TOGETHER, DON'T
YOU THINK?'

Mr Snelly headed down to the roof of Sky Tech to land.

'Dr Brainiov, when were you going to tell us there was a bomb in the next room?'

'Thinking about it now, I should have probably started by saying that.'

'You think?!' Kevin squealed. 'Anything else we should know?'

'Don't worry, it's not activated. If it were, we'd be dead. I mean, toast, completely done for. Maggot food. Ashes blowing in the wind. Grains of—'

'Yes, I get the idea!' Kevin exclaimed. 'You don't need to go on about it.'

'Master, what is this feeling I have? It's like the opposite of lolz 2.0. Why will it not go away?' WALLI sniffled.

'You've scared my trousers—are you happy now?'

THWACK!

What was that noise? Kevin wondered. *It sounded like a crack, but where had it come from and why was the room spinning?* Suddenly Kevin touched the back of his head. It didn't sting, it just felt numb.

'Of course!' Kevin muttered under his breath. 'I've just been hit on the head,' he managed to mumble before collapsing to the ground.

Kevin woke up tied to a chair in the room where he had first jumped through the window. Dr Brainiov sat next to him, with a huge lump on his head.

'This is turning into a really bad day,' Kevin sighed.

'*Au contraire!*' Mr Snelly grinned.

'What does *au contraire* mean?' Kevin asked, his head ringing like an old-fashioned alarm clock.

'It's French for "on the contrary",' Mr Snelly snarled.

'Are you French?' Kevin enquired.

'No.'

'Then why are you speaking French? Oh, do you think *I'm* French?' Kevin wondered, genuinely intrigued.

'NO!' Snelly yelled.

'Well, let's stick to English, shall we?'

'Oh, all right then,' Snelly grimaced. He then pulled the data chip from his pocket. 'With this virus, I can destroy the internet, and the power to rule the world will be MINE! Pretty impressive, isn't it? You have to agree that the good doctor has really excelled himself.' Snelly chuckled.

'Have I had a bang on the head?' Dr Brainiov asked.

'Yes,' said Kevin.

'My brain feels fizzy.'

'Oh no,' Kevin muttered. 'You're going to be no help at all.' He turned back to Mr Snelly. 'So, come on then, let me have it.'

'Let you have what?' Snelly asked.

'I know you're dying to tell me about your plan; how you're going to destroy the world,' Kevin groaned.

'No, I'm not. It doesn't bother me . . .' Snelly said casually.

'Oh, all righ—' Kevin started.

'But, since you insist, I'll tell you everything!' Snelly said excitedly.

'I knew it. Villains are such show-offs,' Kevin said, shaking his head.

'That's such a cliché . . .' Snelly laughed.

'What does cliché mean?' Kevin asked.

'It's French for . . . well, cliché . . .'

'Seriously, what's with you and the French? No one here is French!'

'Be quiet! This virus will change everything. No protection for the banks—it will be like stealing candy from a baby. And all those nuclear warheads left vulnerable. Maybe I'll direct one to this godforsaken town.'

Suddenly there was a loud siren and one of the computers in the back room whirred to life. A shadowy figure appeared on the screen.

'Arrrgh!' Mr Snelly yelled. He was suddenly transformed from an evil villain into a scared schoolboy. 'It's him!'

'SNELLY!!!!' boomed the mysterious voice. Kevin tried to turn round to look properly at the screen but he was too tightly bound to the chair.

'Yes, sir, yes. I'm here, I'm here!' Snelly said, the panic in his voice making it sound shrill and spiky.

'How is the plan coming along, and who are those idiots tied to the chairs?'

'Don't worry about them, sir, they're just a couple of sneaks. I'll deal with them.'

'You better had, or I'll deal with you. And stand up straight when I'm talking to you! Order, manners, and a civilized world; is that too much to ask for? I bet you're showing off, aren't you? Telling everyone what a clever little boy you are.'

'No, NO, I'm NOT!' Snelly insisted.

'He totally is,' Kevin interrupted.

'Shut up, you snitch.'

'I knew it!' the mysterious voice bellowed. 'Come and see me at the end of the day. Now stop larking around and get on with your work. Got it?!' And, with that, the man disappeared and the screen went dead. *Whose voice was that?* Kevin wondered. *It was so familiar* . . .

'You snitch!' Snelly shrieked. 'You were just trying to get me in trouble. It's just like school, déjà vu all over again.'

'You couldn't be more French if you were wearing a beret and eating a baguette on top of the Eiffel Tower!' Kevin shrieked.

'Stop being mean to me!' Snelly shouted.

'Oh, I'm sorry, I didn't mean to be rude. Must be the blow to the head. I hope I didn't hurt your fist with my bony old skull,' Kevin said sarcastically.

'You'll never get away with this, you two!' Brainiov piped up, looking at Snelly.

'There's only one of him,' Kevin said.

The doctor tried to uncross his eyes, but the effort made him pass out again.

'Before I go and complete my dastardly plan, I need to destroy all evidence of Sky Tech so I'm going to blow you all up!'

Brainiov woke up briefly and yelled, 'You monster!'

'I am, aren't I? It's marvellous!'

'Why are you doing this?' Kevin asked, desperately playing for time. 'What's the internet ever done to you?'

'Oh, I don't care about the internet, but with my hands on the world's money and every government secret, I'll be the most powerful man in all of history!'

'But we need the internet!' Kevin said.

'What, so you can play stupid games on it all day?' Snelly laughed.

'No. Is that really what you think kids use it for? It's a world of knowledge. The internet is a blank piece of paper; it's a silly joke, or it's $E=mc^2$, it's a poem or a news story that will change your life. Just because you don't like what's written up there doesn't mean you get to rip it up. It doesn't belong to you. It doesn't belong to anyone—that's the amazing thing about it.'

'Are you going to be long?' Snelly said impatiently. 'I'm kind of on the clock here.'

'You won't win—guys like you never do,' Kevin said confidently.

'Really? Well, good luck getting out of this one,' Snelly said, before pulling a remote control out of his pocket and hitting a big red button on it.

The bomb ticked into life and began its countdown.

'Prepare to say goodbye, small fry!' Snelly gloated. 'Enjoy your last ten minutes on earth.'

15

WE ARE FAMILY

Suddenly there was a huge crash as the door burst
open in a cloud of smoke, knocking Snelly to the
ground.

'That's right, guess who's back!' Elle said, cracking
her knuckles. 'Nobody ties up my little brother and
threatens to kill him except me!'

'Elle! You're the best big sister in the world.
Good work, WALLI,' Kevin said, looking down at his
trousers.

'Right, what's going on? Who's the sleepy dude?'
Elle said, looking at Snelly lying on the floor.

'That's an evil villain who wants to kill us and destroy the world,' Kevin said.

'Well, how very boring. Destroying the world was sooooo last year,' Elle said, untying the ropes around Kevin and Dr Brainiov.

'Also there's a big bomb in that room over there and I have talking trousers now.'

'Rightio,' Elle said unfazed, noticing the remote control that had been knocked out of Snelly's hand.

'Now, with most bombs, there's usually a set of wires, of various colours. The key is to cut the right colour wire: only then will you be able to defuse the bomb,' Kevin lectured.

'Done it,' Elle said smugly.

'What? How?' Kevin said surprised.

'I just pressed the big red button on the remote that this guy dropped.' Elle turned round to where Snelly was lying, but he wasn't there. He was standing upright, pointing a huge gun at all three of them.

'*Bonjour!*' Snelly yelled, waving the loaded gun in his hand.

'I ONLY SPEAK ENGLISH, MR FRENCH MAN!' Elle yelled back.

'Not you too! For the last time, I'm not French! Now go and stand over there with the other two. Just imagine the headlines: mad scientist and computer hackers found after factory explosion,' Snelly said.

'You'll have trouble detonating that bomb since I have the remote,' Elle said, waving it at Snelly.

'There's more than one way to destroy a factory. Fire, for instance,' said Snelly, smiling.

BRRRRIIIIING!

'One second,' Snelly said, looking apologetic. He pulled out a phone from his pocket and sighed. 'Yes. Hello. Look, I said just wait in the helicopter. Daddy has some business to do. I'm on my way now. No, now. I swear I'd be on my way if I wasn't talking to you right now. No, I won't take you to McDonald's. We're going away from here, somewhere no one will find us, just for a bit until things calm down. Just think of it like a big holiday, but a holiday in which we have to stay indoors hiding all the time and we can't speak to anyone ever. Think of all the quality time you and I will get to spend together, darling. Darling? Why are you sobbing?'

'I don't believe it! You brought your daughter to a kidnapping?' Kevin exclaimed.

'It's not my fault it was "bring your daughter to

work" day. I didn't check my diary!' Snelly pouted, 'and why am I even explaining myself to you?' Snelly pointed the gun at a box full of electrical cables and fired. They sparked and ignited.

'Have fun!' Snelly yelled, edging out of the door. Then there was a clunking sound as it locked. Elle ran over to the door and pulled with all her might, but it didn't budge. She looked round to see the fire spreading wildly already.

'How are we going to get out of here?' Elle said.

'That's the only doorway,' the doctor gasped.

Kevin looked around the large room. 'Yes, but that's not the only way out,' he said, looking at the window, high up in the wall. 'WALLI, can we make it?'

`'Yes, master. In theory I can make the jump, but I don't know if the material's strong enough to carry passengers.'`

'Well, there's only one way to find out,' Kevin said, grinning.

'Find out what?' Elle and Dr Brainiov said, looking at each other anxiously.

'Hold on tight!' Kevin said. He reached out and grabbed Elle's hand. Then he did the same to Dr Brainiov's. 'Hold on to my sleeves.' Kevin looked at the fire, which was raging by now.

'GO FOR IT, WALL||||||!!!!' he commanded.

Kevin's suit leapt up in the air, taking Kevin, Elle, and Dr Brainiov with it, through the clouds of smoke and through the smashed window where Kevin had made his heroic entrance only a few minutes before. Kevin could feel the stitching on the sleeve of his suit ripping; he closed his eyes and hoped that it would last a few more moments. Out through the window they flew.

'How do we land?' Elle squealed.

'Big springs on my feet, of course!' Kevin said as they fell towards the ground before doing a big boing up in the air again.

'Look!' Elle screamed, pointing at the sky. 'Snelly's escaping!'

THE GREAT ESCAPE

Outside the Sky Tech building, Elle, Kevin, and Dr Brainiov got used to the feeling of ground beneath their feet once more. Snelly's helicopter rose beyond the buildings and began to disappear into the distance.

'Great! We've lost him. What now?' Elle stamped her foot in frustration.

'WALLI, can we jump after him?' Kevin asked.

'Sorry, master, I'm afraid he's too far away. But my sensors are picking up another helicopter in the vicinity.'

There was a roar from above as another chopper descended from the clouds. It was P!

'Follow that helicopter—Snelly's inside!' Kevin yelled. 'And get this poor man an ambulance!' Kevin said, pointing at a wobbly-looking Brainiov.

'Hop aboard and we'll get after him!' Shouted P.

Kevin and Elle scrambled into the hovering helicopter and it took off into the sky.

'Good work, agent. We intercepted an alarm call from your trousers that you might be in danger.'

'Snelly's plan is to destroy the internet—he's got a computer virus that's unbreakable. If it finds its way onto a computer, it'll infect everything, and the internet will disappear into a big black hole. He wants to break into every bank in the world and steal all their cash and take control of every nuclear warhead too. He's got the virus with him on a data chip, so we have to stop him getting near a computer.'

'Good work, 006 and a half!' P said, smiling.

'There's something else: there's someone he's working for, someone who's pulling all the strings.

If we follow Snelly, he'll lead us to the real mastermind of this operation.'

Suddenly there was a crack and a whistle from outside the helicopter.

'They're firing at us!' P bawled. 'Here, take the wheel. By the way, who's the girl?'

'Take the wheel? What are you talking about, take the wheel?' Kevin shouted, grabbing the controls as the helicopter lurched in between the buildings.

'I need to return fire, or we're done for!' P yelled. 'Just fly the damn thing!'

'I can't fly a helicopter!' Kevin screamed. I mean, he *really* screamed. Like a little toddler. Kevin's voice went up at least three octaves.

'But you're the best pilot we've got, 006 and a half,' P screamed back.

'Kevin, if you fly this helicopter, I'm telling Mum and Dad,' Elle shouted.

'006 and a half—who is this girl? And who is Kevin?'

'OK, long story . . .' Kevin pulled up, narrowly avoiding a lamp post. 'This is my sister, Elle. I'm not a secret agent, I'm a schoolboy. Jake Pond and I swapped places and I wanted to tell you, but I just got a bit carried away. You're not mad, are you?' Kevin asked.

'But . . . but you look just like 006 and a half,' P said, popping off another couple of shots at the chopper in front.

'I know we look the same—I mean, he has a deeper voice and slightly more stubble than me, but—yeah—funny old world, isn't it?' Kevin replied with a grin.

'I've just put a child in charge of stopping a madman and flying a helicopter. This is a health and safety nightmare!'

'Have I or have I not cracked the case?' Kevin said, folding his arms in defiance.

'NOOOOO!' P and Elle screamed.

'Oh, crikey. Probably shouldn't let go of the controls, should I? Soz, everyone.'

'Yes, yes, I suppose you have . . .' P admitted.

'Well, then, I suggest we all get over the fact that I'm a schoolboy and let me do what I do best . . .'

'Burp your name after drinking a big glass of lemonade?' Elle asked, slightly confused.

'No, not that! Being a spy! My name's Twigg. Kevin Twigg. And I've got a licence to get all up in your face.'

'I know I'm going to regret this . . . Kevin, grab the gun and let me take the controls. It looks as though Snelly's heading for the coast,' P yelled.

'DAD! WHAT ON EARTH IS GOING ON? YOU PROMISED ME A PONY!' Alesha shouted, as her dad leant out of the window and, clinging on to the steering wheel with his knees, fired back towards the helicopter in hot pursuit.

'You know what? Just SHUT UP! For once, shut up about ponies. I'm in the middle of something important here! If you asked me for a diamond-encrusted unicorn that trumped rainbows, I'd buy you one. You want me to throw you a party, I throw you the best in town. I do everything for you, and all you do is gripe! You're like a volcano of nonsense, spouting hot loud noise all day and getting on everyone's nerves, so, for the love of crikey, just let me concentrate or we'll end up in jail!'

'JAIL!' Alesha yelled.

'Yes, jail. I'm sorry to break this to you, dear, but believe it or not, I'm not actually a florist as you thought.'

'What?'

'How many florists do you know with a yacht and houses all over the world?'

'I just thought you were just very good at your job!' Alesha cried.

'Oh, and here come the waterworks. I am very good at my job, my job being a master criminal. I'm excellent, in fact. Well, I was, up until about half an hour ago.'

'Be careful, Kevin!' Elle screamed. 'Snelly's daughter is in that helicopter too, remember.'

'Don't worry,' Kevin called. 'Alesha is in no danger at all. I literally have no chance of hitting that helicopter. I'm a really bad shot!' Kevin explained. 'So far I've taken out two seagulls and made one fisherman very cross. SORRY ABOUT YOUR BOAT, SIR!'

The two helicopters twisted and turned through the sky, following the coastline. Every so often, Snelly's helicopter lurched as he hung out the side to fire at the helicopter behind.

'I HOPE YOU REALIZE HOW MUCH THIS IS GOING TO COST YOU IN THERAPY!' Alesha shrieked at her father.

'Be quiet and get ready; we're going to land,' Snelly ordered.

'Look!' Kevin said, pointing into the distance. 'There's a yacht down there with a helipad—they're heading there to land. P, do you think you can land us on that yacht?' Kevin asked.

'There won't be enough room for two helicopters on there. It might tip the boat into the sea.'

'What are we going to do?' Elle yelled.

Kevin looked around for inspiration and spotted the helicopter's harpoon gun. 'I've got an idea,' He shouted. 'I can zip-wire across.'

'Are sure you can make it?' P replied.

Kevin's brain flashed with doubt for a second. 'Yes, I'm sure.'

'I'll fire the wire; you get ready,' said P. 'Just call me when you need me to pick you up.'

Kevin turned to his sister. She had her earphone and headset on and she was looking out of the window at the waves below.

'Elle, I know we've had our differences, but how about we put them behind us, and we go and get this bad guy together? As a team. I know things haven't always been easy. Perhaps it was your fault, perhaps it was my fault, perhaps it was your fault. We'll never really know. But over the last few days, I can see that you always have my best interests at heart. Who knows what will happen when we land—maybe it'll all go wrong, but I know this much for sure—this evil plot is bigger than us and we have to stop it. I know that you'll have my back and I'll have yours, because we're family, and perhaps I don't say it often enough. But I love you. Now what say you and I go and save this little ol' planet we call home?'

P wiped a tear away from his eye and nodded at Kevin. He was right—Kevin was the perfect man for the job.

Elle turned round and stared deeply into Kevin's eyes and smiled. Then she took off her earphones, grabbed him by the hand, and said, 'These things are great—you can pick up the top forty on the radio station. Man, that was a good tune. Right, are you ready, you little twerp? Let's go and bang some heads together.'

190

17

WE ARE SAILING

FLUUUUUMP!

The line shot out of the harpoon gun and stuck into the deck of Snelly's yacht. Kevin grabbed a rope and looped it over the wire—it all had an alarming sense of familiarity to it. He took a deep breath and remembered where it all began. How everyone had laughed at him. He felt that heave in his belly, a mixture of nerves and embarrassment. What if he failed again? Except this time things were different. Now he was a spy, whether he liked it or not. He might have found himself here by accident but this was his world now. He'd been playing the part of a secret agent for so long that it wasn't a role any more; it was him.

'Kevin, I'm scared,' Elle said.

'You'll be fine! You're the bravest person I know. You just have to believe in yourself a bit more.'

'I'm . . . er . . . sorry I didn't believe in you, Kevin,' Elle mumbled.

Kevin grinned and took Elle's hand. 'Let's do it.'

Kevin and Elle held on to the rope and leapt out of the side of the helicopter as it danced around in the wind. They swung down towards the yacht. Kevin closed his eyes tightly, tucked his knees into his chest, and let go of the rope. He somersaulted through the air and landed perfectly on deck. He'd done it, he'd actually done it! Elle followed shortly

behind, her gymnastics training meaning that she landed safely too, although Kevin thought doing a bow at the end of her dismount was a little over the top.

While Kevin had been preparing for the most daring zip-wire attempt of his life, Snelly had already landed and dashed below deck to upload the virus. He grabbed his laptop and hit the start button. Nothing happened.

'Why isn't this working?' Snelly screamed.

'Oh . . . erm . . .' Alesha looked at her feet.

'WHAT HAVE YOU DONE?'

'It wasn't my fault, I swear.'

'What wasn't your fault?'

'So I was totally doing my homework on it the other day; I'd been working for hours on this assignment, because I'm, like, totally a committed student and I just want to make my dear dad happy, because I love him, like, for real and everything. I decided to take a break, so I got myself, like, a drink of water or milk or something really healthy, and went on the internet and was, like, looking at something really serious, like Shakespeare or maybe some maths—something really important like that—when from nowhere this cat video popped up. I mean, it was so stupid and pathetic, yet also totally hilarious too, and I laughed, I mean I did a ROFL and everything and knocked over my refreshing yet healthy drink, and I think the computer might have broken or something. I dunno, but it wasn't my fault at all . . . I'm like totes sorry, Dad,' Alesha said with a forced smile.

'You've ruined me.' Snelly stared into the distance. 'It's over.'

'Sorry, Dad.'

'Oh, shut up, you annoying teenager. The only consolation is that when I go to jail I'll get a break from you.'

'How can you be so mean?' Alesha sobbed.

'Oh great, here come the waterworks again . . .'

'I'm totally going to tell everyone you said that. Let's see what Facebook makes of your meanness!' Alesha yelled, grabbing her phone and dabbing her eyes with a tissue.

'Your phone, of course! I have the virus; all I need to do is open it on your phone and upload it!' Snelly grabbed Alesha's phone and frantically shoved the data chip in. 'No mobile data! How have you managed to use up all your data allowance? It's only the beginning of the month!' Snelly yelled.

'Oh yeah, sorry, Dad, I was on YouTube watching a funny thing when they texted me to tell me that I'd used it all up. I meant to say.'

'Text!' Snelly's eyes lit up. 'That's it! I text the virus to the boss and he can open it up.'

Snelly made a call and waited impatiently while it rang. 'Answer it, you silly old fool, Ahhh . . . hello, yes, it's me. Listen, there's a problem, sir. I'm going text you the virus. All you have to do is open the link I'm texting to you now. No, I'll text it to your phone. No, not this phone, the mobile one I gave you, remember? Yes, yes, I know you don't like phones, but I can't get online here to do it myself. Well, going online means . . . oh, listen, I don't have time for this now. All you have to do is this one simple thing: ONE. SIMPLE. THING. Open the link on the text I'm sending you on your mobile phone. Or everything will be ruined! You do know how to turn it on—I showed you, about five hundred times. No,

I'm not being cheeky,' Snelly said, looking up at the fast-approaching helicopter. 'Turn the phone on, click on the text, and open the link. Then the virus will be everywhere!'

'You know what I really hate, sis?' Kevin smirked, entering the room with Elle by his side.

'Broccoli?' Elle answered.

'Well, yes, that's true, I do hate broccoli.'

Snelly pressed send and quickly dropped the phone over the side of the boat.

'I mean, I like how it looks like a little tree, but that's the only good thing about it. No, the thing I really hate is people who think they can get away with whatever they like. Stealing from banks, for example, or hitting people over the head. Oh yes, and people who think that they can destroy the internet. That really gets my goat,' Kevin said.

'But what kind of yacht-owning, head-hitting, French-speaking, poo-poo head would do that?' Elle said casually.

'The internet?' Alesha cried. 'You were going to destroy the internet?'

'Hush now,' Snelly snapped before turning to face Kevin and Elle. 'And stop calling me poo-poo head!'

'Why, Mr Poo-Poo Head, don't you like your name?' Kevin said.

'SHUT UP! YOU'RE THE POO-POO HEADS!' Snelly yelled.

'I know you are, but what am I?' Elle replied.

'No, you're the poo-poo head.'

'I know you are, but what am I?'

'You won't win at this,' Kevin said, chuckling.

'You're just a pair of idiotic kids, you can't stop me.'

'I know you are, but what am I?' Elle repeated, grinning.

'Arrrgh, stop it!' Snelly wept.

'Wait, I know you—you came to my party,' Alesha said, pointing at Kevin.

'Yes, yes, I did . . . how enchanting that you remembered,' Kevin said, wiggling his eyebrows up and down. 'I work for Her Majesty's Secret Service. I have a licence to kill and you have a licence to thrill . . . me, I mean.'

'Kevin, work to do!' Elle said, nudging him in the ribs.

'Weren't you a real idiot at the party? I mean, horribly nerdy and strangely geeky?' Alesha asked.

'I was deep undercover. That was an act, but this is the real me. Now give me a few moments to apprehend your father and then let's go get a milkshake.'

'You're too late!' Snelly declared. 'I've already sent the virus to my boss. Order, manners, and a civilized world, that's the future! Ha!'

'I can't believe you are going to kill the internet!' Alesha screamed at her father.

'I'm doing this all for you!' Snelly shouted back at her.

'For me?'

'Yes, Alesha—we'll be rich! With no computers, the banks will be ours for the taking. All the things you want come at a price, you know!'

'How dare you blame this on me? I didn't make you do anything! I hate you!'

'Perhaps we could trace the number on the phone?' Elle said to Kevin.

'Well, I hope you're a good swimmer!' Snelly chuckled, looking over the side.

'Oh no, he's thrown it overboard. That's it, game over! What are we going to do? There's no way to find out who he sent the virus to!' Elle gasped, as she looked at the swirling sea below.

But Kevin's mind was busy ticking over. *Order, manners, and a civilized world . . .* He'd heard those words before, but where? Then it hit him—finally the last piece of the puzzle had fallen into place.

'I know exactly who Snelly's boss is!' Kevin said. 'We need to go—now.'

'But what about him?' Elle said pointing at Snelly.

THUD!

Alesha rubbed her hands together and put what remained of the broken vase on the side. Snelly had been knocked out cold.

'No one—and I mean no one—takes away my amusing videos of cats playing the piano. Not on my watch. Let's go!'

18

RUN

Kevin grabbed his watch and barked into it.

'P, we need the helicopter now. I know who the boss is. We're going back to school.'

'School...? Kevin, what's going on?' Elle shouted, as she ran to the top of the deck.

'I'll explain on the way,' Kevin bellowed, seeing the helicopter hovering above them.

'How are we going to get on board?' Alesha asked.

'With my magic trousers, of course,' Kevin said. 'We're going for a bit of a ride! WALLI?'

'I'm right here, Kevin,' Walli's robotic voice shouted.

'Did your—?' Alesha started.

'Yes, they did,' Kevin answered smirking. 'I'm all about the gadgets. Right, you two ready?'

Alesha and Elle looked at each other and nodded.

'WALLI, get us on board that helicopter!'

'Yeah, baby!' Walli cried, before springing the three of them up into the air and in through the open door.

'Whhhhaaaaaa!' Elle and Alesha whooped, exhilarated. 'We did it!'

'Where's Snelly?' P asked.

'His daughter just smashed him over the head with a very expensive vase!' Elle explained.

'Pleased to meet you,' Alesha mouthed to P.

'Good golly, you mean Snelly fell on his belly after his daughter gave him a welly? Cripes!' P exclaimed. 'Right, where are we going?'

'To my school,' Kevin said firmly.

'To your school?!' everyone, including Kevin's trousers.

'Yes, it came to me when Snelly was talking about his boss. He kept saying, "Order, manners, and a civilized world", and I knew I'd heard it somewhere before. Alesha, where did your dad go to school?'

'He went to St Peter's, I think. It was in the town where he was born.'

'I knew it. Elle and I go to the same school,' Kevin explained. 'And there's only one teacher who would have been around back then, and only one teacher who hates computers so much that he wants to destroy the internet. Mr Plunk. He said those exact words to me only a few days ago. *Order, manners, and a civilized world*. Your dad, Mr Snelly, is doing it all for him. He's the only person that a criminal mastermind would be terrified of. He's still trying to get into his good books after all these years.'

'Why, Kevin, that's brilliant. You've cracked the case!' P exclaimed in delight.

'Not yet. Mr Snelly sent him the virus. All Mr Plunk has to do is turn on his phone, and activate it. The good news is, I don't think Mr Plunk has ever turned on a mobile phone in his life. He was sent the virus about twenty minutes ago so I reckon he might have found the "on" button by now.'

'Bingo! I've finally found the on button. It only took twenty minutes and some top-level swearing to turn on this ridiculous phone. Now what did that snivelling little wretch of a pupil of mine say? I have to open the telegram, click on the link, and send the disease—I mean—virus that will infect everyone.'

Just then Mr Plunk 's office door burst open. It was the English teacher, Mrs Frink.

'Errr, sir, they're ready for you. The talent show is about to start,' she said nervously.

'Oh really, do I have to attend? There's nothing worse than a bunch of soppy teenagers showing off,' he griped, shoving the phone into his pocket.

Mr Plunk and Mrs Frink bounded down the corridor towards the hall. It was packed with parents and siblings, all keen to see their loved ones on stage. I say *keen,* I obviously mean obliged. But you get the idea. Mr and Mrs Twigg were sitting in the front row, delighted that their son was apparently a poetry genius. What they still didn't know was that the person they thought was their son was really a secret agent on holiday as he couldn't cope with all the murdering and killing that he'd been doing for the last twenty years. That's murdering for you: really takes it out of you.

'Do you know what his poem is about?' Kevin's dad asked his wife.

'No idea—he wouldn't tell me. All I heard was the wailing of despair as he tapped into the emotional reservoir of his torment.'

'Not going to be a funny limerick about bottoms then?' Dad said with disappointment.

Mrs Frink tapped the microphone to get everyone's attention. 'Welcome to St Peter's annual talent show. First on stage is a pupil who has been hiding his tremendous gift for poetry underneath the mask of being an incompetent nerd. Master Kevin Twigg!'

The lights went down until it was pitch black and then, from the ceiling above, a single spotlight illuminated a tiny area at the centre of the stage. Jake Pond slid on his knees across the stage, coming to a halt beneath the light. With his eyes closed, his fist clenched, he began . . .

'Life . . . is empty, like a bubble of hate. I am the bubble, you are the hate . . .'

High above the town Kevin and the gang finally had the school in their sights.

'There it is, P. Can you bring us down on the playing field?'

'Yes, no problem. What's the plan?'

'Land, serve a family-sized portion of whoop-ass, then home in time for tea and toast.'

'Excellently vague, but I suppose it'll have to do. Good luck, Agent!' P smiled.

'You mean Kevin.'

'No, I mean agent.'

' . . . am the fly in your soup of death. The killing, all the killing, why can't I stop killing all the people I am killing?' Jake Pond continued, as the tears ran down his face.

Mum whispered to Dad, 'Do you think Kevin's all right? Do you think we might need to call a doctor?'

'Or the police?' Dad said, gulping. 'Is this a poetry reading or a confession?'

' . . . I am an empty shell, where once feelings lived, died, cried, spied . . .'

The audience groaned in unison, while Mrs Frink gently dabbed her eyes.

The dramatic ending to Jake's poem was interrupted when the school hall doors burst open. Kevin, Elle, and Alesha ran in. The audience gasped, not least Mr and Mrs Twigg, who were rather shocked by the sight of two Kevins in the same room.

'What are you doing here?' Jake Pond whispered. 'You're breaking our cover.'

'No time to explain. Where's Plunk?' Kevin said, running on to the stage.

'Oh hi, Mum and Dad, I'm a spy now. And that's not your real son,' he said, pointing at Jake.

'What's going on?' Mr Plunk squawked. 'Why are there two of you?'

'Aha!' Didn't see that coming, did you?' Kevin laughed.

'If you're there, who have I been listening to read awful poetry for the last forty minutes?'

'Hey, I was good!' Jake yelled.

'Oh, it was terrible. Am I right?' Plunk exclaimed gesturing to the audience.

'Don't listen to him,' Mrs Frink shouted, jumping out of her seat.

'What did you call my poetry?' Jake said with a steely glare.

'You heard,' Plunk sneered.

Jake Pond pulled out a gun from his inside pocket. 'Mock my poetry again. I dare you. I double dare you.' He pulled the loading mechanism back and pointed the gun at Mr Plunk's head.

'Stop!' Kevin yelled. 'You can't kill someone for not liking your poetry!'

'I've killed for less,' Jake Pond replied dryly.

'OK, still working on the anger issues, I see,' Kevin said, patting Jake on the shoulder.

'Don't do it, whoever you are . . .' Mrs Frink screamed. 'All geniuses are misunderstood; it's what makes them artists.'

Jake Pond slowly uncocked his gun and put it back in his pocket. 'There will be no killing today. The poet is too tired.'

'Will someone please tell me what's going on!' Plunk said, his arms high above his head in frustration.

'May I?' Jake said to Kevin.

'You go ahead,' Kevin replied. 'The stage is yours.'

'I am a spy. I work for a secret organization called MI7 and we keep the world safe. You don't see us; we're an invisible army, we're ghosts. Well, this particular ghost has been doing the job for a long time and I needed to take some time out. That's when I saw Kevin doing his stunt show. Not only was he nimble like a ninja, but he looked exactly like me. We could be twins. So we decided to swap lives for a little while. I get to be a kid, he gets to be a spy. It would have been great, but MI7 had other plans and they made Kevin take one last job. Kevin, do you want to take it from here?'

'I cracked the case and uncovered the identity of the evil villain behind it all: Mr Plunk.'

A loud 'BEEP BEEP' suddenly interrupted everything.

'Right, who's got a phone? No one should have a phone on—you know the school rules,' Mr Plunk bellowed.

'Erm, it came from your pocket, Mr Plunk,' Kevin said.

'What . . . Ooh,' Mr Plunk said, suddenly remembering what was in his pocket.

'What are you doing with a mobile phone?' Kevin asked. 'Wait a sec . . . I bet Snelly gave it to you; who else would text you? It must have only just come through.'

'That's right, I have the virus now. Ha ha ha!' Plunk cackled to himself, pulling the phone out of his pocket.

The crowd gasped. Mr Plunk made a run for it, as best as a man can with a dodgy knee. Kevin leapt after him, tackling Mr Plunk and sending him flying to the ground. The phone shot out of his hands and across the hall. Plunk elbowed Kevin on the nose and dived after the phone. He grinned triumphantly, as he clutched the phone in his hand. 'Nobody move a muscle. One click and I've won!'

Kevin and Jake looked at one another. What could they do now?

19

SMOOTH CRIMINAL

'Go on then, do your worst!' Kevin urged.

Jake Pond looked at Kevin in disbelief. What was he up to?

'It's about time this world listened to me and for too many years I've had to deal with rapscallions and nincompoops,' Plunk snarled.

Stu turned to Pete. 'What's a rapscallion or a nincompoop?'

'Oh, you see? Ignorant, you're all ignorant!' Plunk cried. 'It means you're all awful, terrible people, who don't listen to me, who have bad manners, who cheek me all the time, and I've had enough of it!'

'I don't like this poem at all,' Kevin's dad said. 'It doesn't even rhyme!'

'This isn't a poem, you nincompoop!' Mum hissed through clenched teeth. 'This is for real!'

'Oh, so he's really an evil genius who wants to destroy the world?' Dad sat back in his chair and opened a bag of sucky sweets. 'That does makes more sense.'

'Quiet!' Plunk roared so loudly bits of mouth-gravy flew out of his lips. 'Can't you see I'm doing my evil villain speech? Stop interrupting me and let me finish. Where was I?' he said, scratching his head.

'You've had enough of it all!' one boy cried out.

'Oh, thank you, Smithers, have a house point. Yes, I've had enough of it all. I want to destroy the internet and the world as we know it. I've got my eye on some nuclear warheads with your names on them! How do you like that, you little twerks!'

'I think he means twerps,' Stuart muttered to Peter.

'I wanted to destroy the internet but I didn't know how until my former pupil and criminal mastermind showed up one day. He was happy to help; even after all these years he's still trying to win my approval and get that B for maths.'

'All this so Snelly could get a B in maths?' Kevin asked.

'Pathetic, isn't it? Well, say goodbye to everything that you hold dear, m'dears. I have the thingy m'bob, that I can open to the what's-it-called and that will destroy the whole shebang!'

'Go ahead, Plunk. Make my day!' Kevin replied confidently. The whole room held its breath.

Plunk held the phone aloft and pressed the button on the side. Nothing happened. He pressed it again. Still nothing. Then he grabbed his glasses and put them on, resting them on the tip of his nose.

'Darn thing . . .' he muttered. 'It was working a second ago. Maybe it's cold. If I warm it up a bit in my hands it'll work, or perhaps it needs more signal . . .

yes, that's a thing. If I stand on a chair and rub it on my legs like a cricket ball, it'll work.'

Mr Plunk stood on a wobbly chair at the side of the stage and started to rub the phone on his legs as if he was about to open the bowling for the Grandads' XI.

'Oh, this is so embarrassing,' Kevin said, shaking his head. 'Would you like a hand, sir?'

'Yes—I just need to open the thing that's inside the telegram . . . I think that was it.'

'Your phone is quite old and you were trying to open it with the volume button, sir,' Kevin said, gently taking the phone off Mr Plunk.

'Well, I'm not very good with this technology. I like painting with watercolours and listening to the Sunday afternoon music show on the wireless.'

'Let me see if I can fix it . . . I wonder what this button does? Ah, it means I can telephone someone!' Kevin said, grinning at his headmaster.

'But it's not connected to the wall!'

'I know, it's amazing, isn't it? You know I could have shown you all the things a phone does, or a how computer works. Maybe instead of trying to make everyone listen to you, for a change you could listen to other people? Just because we're different ages, it doesn't mean we can't learn from each other,' Kevin said, handing the phone back to Mr Plunk.

'Oh, hello, is there someone there?' Plunk asked, looking over at Kevin. 'He wants to know where

I am . . . I'M AT ST PETER'S SCHOOL, YOUNG MAN. I told him I'm at St Peter's School,' Mr Plunk said to Kevin.

'Oh, who is it?' Kevin asked.

'Oh, I don't know. WHO IS THIS?' Plunk said politely. 'Oh, it's the police!'

'Oh, the police! How exciting,' Kevin said, grinning and nodding.

'I know! I wonder what they want?' Mr Plunk said, shaking his head in surprise.

'They probably want to arrest you for trying to throw the world into chaos,' Kevin said, chuckling.

'Oh yes—ha ha ha!—you're probably right!' Mr Plunk replied, looking at Kevin and laughing. 'WAIT, WHAT?!' His grin suddenly disappeared from his face. 'You tricked me!' Plunk grabbed the phone and tried to find the virus.

'Oh, I've deleted the message, sir. The game's up.'

At that, Mr Plunk threw the phone to the floor, dashing out of the hall and off along the corridor.

Kevin picked up Plunk's phone and chucked it as hard as he could.

'YOU KNOW THE RULES, SIR. NO RUNNING IN THE CORRIDOR!' Kevin called out. The phone clonked Mr Plunk right on the head and he collapsed like a bag of turnips.

'Cuff him!' P ordered as he ran into the hall, flanked by half a dozen police officers.

The room erupted into huge cheers and then everyone got their phones out to check the internet was still working, and it was. Facebook statuses were updated with 'The world has been saved, lol'. Jake Pond ran over to congratulate Kevin as did his sister, mum, and dad. Kevin Twigg was no longer a joke. He was the coolest kid in school.

Kevin fought his way through the cheering crowd to find Alesha standing near the door. 'Hey, Alesha, it must be a weird day, finding out that your dad was plotting to destroy the world,' Kevin said, trying to comfort her.

'Yeah, lots of things are beginning to make sense now . . . Like why he wanted a bulletproof vest for Christmas instead of a woolly pullover; why he was the only florist in the world who had a missile launcher in the back garden. Maybe I was a bit spoilt, but we can spend time working through our issues when I visit him in jail, I suppose. Anyway, you gonna buy me that milkshake now?' Alesha smiled at Kevin, putting her arm on his shoulder.

'How do you like it?' Kevin said, raising an eyebrow.

'I like milkshakes, like I like my men . . .' she giggled. 'Extra thick!'

'Yeah, baby . . . wait, what?' Kevin said, scratching his head.

Alesha just laughed.

TO THE END

Kevin woke up in his own bed. Things had been back to normal for a couple of months now, but it still felt great to be home. For the thousandth time he wondered for a second if it had all been a cheese-induced dream . . .

'Good morning, Kevin.'

Kevin looked over at the trousers hanging on the back of his chair. 'Good morning, WALLI. And how are you?'

'I am very well, thank you. I was just thinking how much more fun

it is being here rather on a spy's
legs. Think of all that running
and jumping . . . and, as we know,
spies do have a tendency to wet
themselves.'

'Indeed they do, WALLI. Right, shall we get
dressed and go and have some breakfast? I'm in the
mood for vast quantities of food.'
Kevin was tucking into his second round of cheese
on toast when he heard a loud rumble from above.

'What on earth's that?' Dad yelled.

'Sounds like a helicopter!' Mum said.

'Must be P!' Kevin said, going to the window to watch the helicopter landing in the back garden.

'My pansies!' Kevin's dad squealed.

P leaned out of the window and looked down at the squished plants below the helicopter.

'Sorry, old bean! Kevin, do you want a lift to school?' P called out.

'Sure . . . shall I fly?' Kevin suggested.

'Yeaaaah . . . nah,' P said, smiling. 'Maybe next time.'

The helicopter zoomed high above Kevin's house. It was strange to see his town from up here. It was so familiar, but looked so different from the sky. Kevin had decided that perhaps the place wasn't so bad after all. He used to think it was boring, but a place is what you make it—if you look, there's adventure lurking around any corner. No one knew that better than Kevin.

'Did you see the news?' P asked.

'Yes, Mr Plunk is going to be spending a long time in jail. Still, at least he'll be in a place where there's order and, obedience. Have you heard from Jake lately?'

'He's got himself a new career as a beat poet. The critics love him. Maybe Mrs Frink was right about Jake all along, although it could be something to do with the fact that he's threatened to kill any critic who gives him a bad review.'

The helicopter touched down in the playing field. Kevin was about to grab his school bag and jump out, when P put his hand on Kevin's shoulder. He handed Kevin a gift-wrapped box and card.

'Just a little something to say thank you, and my card. If ever you need a job, give me a call. There's room for more than one Twigg in the Service.'

Kevin grinned and opened the box. It wasn't; it couldn't be . . . !

'No way, he never said that?' Stu and Pete said in unison.

'He did, just now!' Kevin said, showing them P's card.

'He gave me one of these too,' Kevin said, holding up his brand new MiPhone25.

'You got one!' Pete and Stu exclaimed.

'Yep, sireeee!' Kevin replied smugly.

'I'm getting a MiPhone26 for my birthday so we can be phone buddies,' added Stu, grinning.

'What?' Kevin scowled.

'Yeah, it's just come out.'

'Oh noooooo.' Kevin shoulders slumped. 'I guess I'm going to have to start saving again.'

Later that day, Kevin and his friends were walking home. 'Hey, Kevin, what's Elle up to these days?' Pete asked 'We never see her around any more.'

'Oh, she's around. Still getting in people's way, annoying them, the usual.' Kevin smiled to himself. 'Enough talking, anyway—it's time to think about a new stunt show. Especially now there's a new phone to save up for.'

Kevin pulled a book out of his bag and handed it to Stu. 'I've been thinking about this one for a while now. I'm thinking a bungee rope and small paddling pool . . . what do you think?'

'Are you sure bungee jumping off Big Ben is a good idea, Kevin?' asked Stu, glancing at the book.

'Of course! What could possibly go wrong?' Kevin replied. 'You do the posters, I'll get my costume ready. It'll be all over the internet this time next week!'

Meanwhile in a Siberian prison . . .

'Who are you and what do you want?' whimpered a man, who sat tied to a chair inside a dark concrete cell.

'I want to know the truth, you little twerp, the truth,' the voice calmly responded.

'Who . . . who are you?' he sobbed.

'The name is Elle, and I've got a licence to get all up in your grill.'

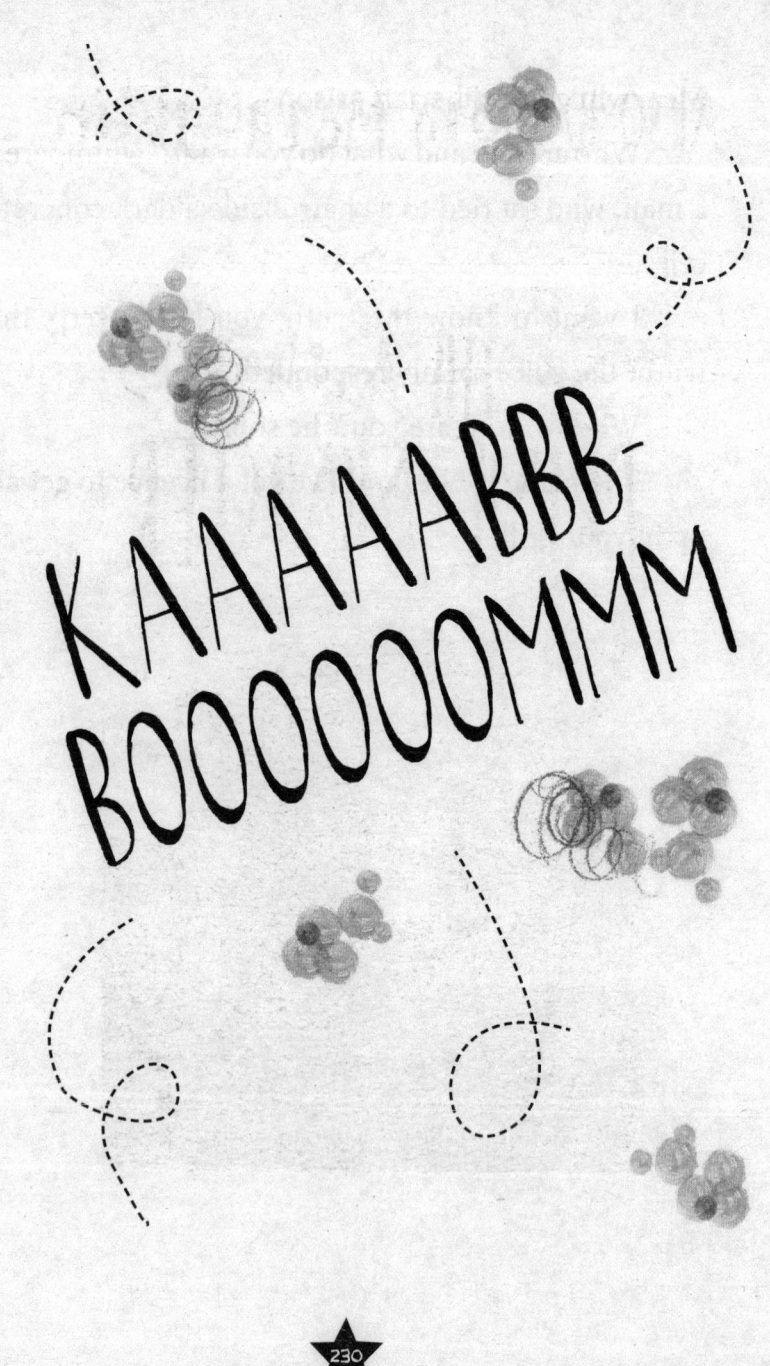

KAAAAABBB-
BOOOOOOOMMM

ALSO BY **Tom McLaughlin**

ABOUT THE AUTHOR

Before becoming a writer and illustrator, Tom spent nine years working as a political cartoonist for *The Western Morning News*, thinking up silly jokes about even sillier politicians. In 2004 Tom took the plunge and began illustrating and writing his own books. Since then he has written and illustrated fiction and picture books as well as working on animated TV shows for Disney and Cartoon Network.

Tom lives in Devon and his hobbies include drinking tea, looking out of the window, and eating biscuits. *The Accidental Secret Agent* is the follow-up to his debut children's novel *The Accidental Prime Minister*.

READY FOR MORE GREAT STORIES? TRY ONE OF THESE . . .

MR BABOOMSKI AND THE WONDER GOAT

DANNY DREAD

THE DEMON HEADMASTER

ELECTRIGIRL